I0690573

PLUM BLOSSOM'S FRAGRANT LOINS

A Free Re-Telling of Lanling Xiaoxiao Sheng's
Jin Ping Mei, *A Classic Chinese Erotic Tale*

First Edition

Published by the Nazca Plains Corporation
Las Vegas, Nevada
2014

ISBN: 978-1-61098-241-2
E-Book: 978-1-61098-242-9

Published by
The Nazca Plains Corporation ®
4640 Paradise Rd, Suite 141
Las Vegas NV 89109-8000

PUBLISHER'S NOTE
Plum Blossom's Fragrant Loins is a work of fiction created wholly by *Tim Desmondes'* imagination. All characters are fictional and any resemblance to any persons living or deceased is purely by accident. No portion of this book reflects any real person or events.

Cover Image, Oriartiste
Art Director, Blake Stephens

DEDICATION

This book is dedicated to those readers who appreciate the difference between erotica and pornography.

Serious readers of erotica are well acquainted with European authors like Ovid, de Sade, von Sacher-Masoch, and Miller. The oriental masterpieces are not as easily accessible to these aficionados.

I have relied on Clement Egerton's 1955 translation of the *Jin Ping Mei* from the Chinese into English and on Ramakrishna Das Gupta's 1963 translation into Hindi as the basis of my retelling.

So I dedicate this free retelling in English of the *Jin Ping Mei* to those who wish to go beyond the Western genre and sample a masterpiece of Chinese erotica.

Tim Desmondes

PLUM BLOSSOM'S FRAGRANT LOINS

A Free Re-Telling of Lanling Xiaoxiao Sheng's
Jin Ping Mei, *A Classic Chinese Erotic Tale*

First Edition

Tim Desmondes

CONTENTS

INTRODUCTION

Pearl Buck wrote that *Jin Pin Mei* was "China's greatest novel of physical love." And that same novel was Mao Zedong's favorite book. It was written in the Qing Dynasty and is set in the Song Dynasty (960-1279 AD).

The novel has appeared over the years in several different versions, all telling the same tale. The title has been translated as "The Plum in the Golden Vase", "Golden Lotus" and "Plum Blossom's Fragrant Loins". The last title was used in an early Indian translation into Hindi and is one of the sources of the following English translation.

An early translation into English – in 1979 – was by Clement Egerton. But there was an even earlier translation, which was privately published.

Soon after its publication in China, an Indian by the name of Ramakrishna Das Gupta translated it into Hindi and thenceforth into English and it was privately printed in Bombay (present day

Mumbai) in 1963.   That translation was quite widely read, but was soon repressed outside of India because it violated copyright laws. However, copies are still available in English book booths in Mumbai bazaars.

Das Gupta's translation was titled *Plum Blossom's Fragrant Loins*, and was also published in Bombay, and a number of copies found their way to England.

The few extant copies are considered collectors' items.

I have relied heavily on both Egerton's and Das Gupta's translations to retell the story for contemporary readers.

Tim Desmondes

THE ARRIVAL OF THE TIGER SLAYER

It was Wu Pu's wedding day.

Pu was a peddler of buns and pies who was ugly, stunted in growth and disfigured. He was a man of modest means who could afford a part-time cook named Mother Fu, and a servant girl, Ling Ling. And when the time came for him to marry, he was able to afford to buy a comely wife for himself.

Master Po, the city's marriage broker, had available a very beautiful bride. Beautiful, yes. But urmarketable. She was a virago with a disposition that had turned away client after client. Her name was Plum Blossom.

Since it was beauty that Wu Pu sought, and beauty only, he was able to negotiate a price within his means for the gorgeous woman of his dreams.

So on his wedding day, it was Plum Blossom who followed him – disgruntled – to his modest home.

When the newlywed couple went to the bedroom, the bride clearly and unequivocally refused to grant Pu any conjugal rights whatsoever. Pu was both a modest and a timid man and granted her sole possession of the bed while he settled for a floor mat in the corner.

Few, if any, men in the province would have settled for such an arrangement. But Wu Pu was unfortunate enough to see himself as others saw him. He had a beautiful wife and he was content.

Not long after the marriage, a military man came knocking at the door. When she answered, Plum Blossom's heart gave a little leap. For standing there on the other side of the door was a tall, strikingly handsome uniformed man. The soldier's left hand rested on a lethal-looking iron club.

The imposing visitor was a stranger to Plum Blossom but no stranger to the house. For he was none other than Wu Pu's younger brother, Wu Hung.

Wu Pu's younger brother, Wu Hung – unlike Pu himself – was handsome, vigorous, and strong. As a young man, he had no interest in following the family bun peddling business and went off to fend for himself on King Yang Mountain.

A quick glance immediately informed Plum Blossom that the officer was over six feet tall. The musculature that revealed itself within his sleeves proved that his muscles bulged. The outline from behind his regulation official pantaloons revealed that the man was well endowed.

What Plum Blossom could not tell from her superficial observation was this: Hung was an intelligent man, and believed in a simple, vigorous lifestyle. He was a devout Chan Buddhist, and was dedicated to living an honorable life. He was patriotic and was a proud subject of the emperor, the Son of Heaven.

During the years when Wu Hung lived on the remote mountain, exercising his enormous strength and his iron club, he slayed wild animals – tigers, bears, and other ferocious beasts – up in his mountain wilderness.

There on the mountain, he wore only a loincloth and thus, simply clad, he braved the elements without regard for the vicissitudes of the elements.

His fame spread throughout the Middle Kingdom and he was known as The Tiger Slayer of King Yang Mountain.

In due time, his legendary fame reached the ears of General Yong, who felt the empire needed such a man in its armed forces. The general went up onto King Yang Mountain unattended by any guard and talked to the legendary giant.

All it took was for the general to tell that giant that the Son of Heaven required his services. Wu Hung was a devout Buddhist who followed the precepts of Bodhidharma who brought the light across the high mountains to China and founded the Shaolin Temple and Monastery.

One of Bodhdharma's teachings was that one must obediently honor the dictates of his nation. Wu Hung could not refuse the call of the emperor.

Within a very few years of service, Wu Hung rose to the rank of captain.

In due course, the imperial magistrate of the province where the captain was born was in need of a husky giant to guard the yamen, the provincial headquarters.

It was determined that Wu Hung was the very man for the job and he was summoned to return to the province to guard the portals of the yamen with his iron club.

And the mighty captain now appeared at his brother's door to pay a fraternal visit.

When Captain Wu told Plum Blossom that he was Pu's brother and that he had come to pay his respects to his older brother, Plum Blossom informed him that she was Pu's wife and invited him into the house.

She ordered Ling Ling to prepare tea for the visitor and invited Hung to sit at the table with her.

"Your brother is still out in the city selling his wares," she told him. "I expect him back before long. Won't you wait?"

"I have waited for many years now to see my beloved brother again," Hung replied. "I am prepared to wait her for him until his return."

Ling Ling came in with the tea and teacakes and set the tray on the table. Plum Blossom poured.

Her eyes could not get enough of her stunning brother-in-law. After she had told him how happy she was to be his brother's wife and how devoted she was to him, she encouraged him to tell her all about himself. For Pu had never had a chance to say so much as a word about himself and his family to her.

Wu Hung was not given to any kind of reticence in talking about himself. Nor was false modesty a part of his being. So, while they sipped tea and munched on cakes, he told her the highlights of his life from the day he had left the city until his recent return.

To Plum Blossom the tale was more exciting than any heroic story she had ever heard. And, actually, anything the sexy captain had to say would have stirred her heart as mightily.

In due course, Pu returned home from his day of vending pastries, buns and pies. The reunion of the brothers was hearty.

When Pu realized that his brother would truly be living right within the city, he was overjoyed.

"Where are you staying?" he asked.

"In the barracks by the yamen," he was told.

Plum Blossom took the opportunity to exclaim, "You must stay with us, Brother-in-law! Mustn't he Pu Dear?"

Pu was delighted with the idea. And was stunned to hear his beautiful wife address him as "dear."

"Yes, indeed, Brother," he chimed in. "Your sister-in-law is a marvelous cook. And our maid, Ling Ling serves beautifully, as you have probably noted. Do say you will do us the honor of living here. As you will see, we even have an extra bedroom that was meant to serve as a nursery. We are not yet blessed with children, so the room is available for you."

There indeed were no children, for there had been no copulation. And there would not be any. But that was not a matter ever to be discussed.

The thought of living once again with his brother appealed to Hung. So he agreed that he would move in.

"That is wonderful, Brother Hung," Plum Blossom exclaimed. "This calls for a family celebration. Pu, Love. Why don't you run down to the marketplace and bring back some good fresh meat and fish and some vegetables. We already have enough rice here in the kitchen. And, oh yes. A nice crock of tiger bone wine would make the celebration even more festive."

His wife had called him "Pu Love." It seemed to Pu that the arrival of the long lost brother was improving things in the household immensely. So he hurried out as fast as he could equip himself with baskets to carry back the supplies for the party Plum Blossom had proposed.

Plum Blossom knew this was not the occasion to seduce the virile soldier. There would be time enough for that when he had moved in and when Pu would be absent selling his pies for hours at a time. She just wanted to be alone with Hung. She would act submissive the way she wanted to appear to him for the moment.

And as she let her eyes take in his muscled body, she issued a silent prayer of thanks to Lady Chang-o, the goddess of the moon and of love in the Old Religion, which was still very much alive in the Song Dynasty.

During the time of Pu's absence, Plum Blossom and Hung filled the time with polite conversation. Plum Blossom's thoughts and imaginings affected her body in such a way that her crotch remained quite moist. And the female scent that emanated from her love-box wafted about the room.

Wu Hung was possessed of a healthy male libido. He was certainly aware of the spirit of femininity that surrounded him. But the Buddhist teachings so inhabited his soul that he was well armored against any lewd thoughts towards his brother's wife. The stirrings in his body that nature demanded were firmly overridden by the precepts he had accepted from the teachings of Bodhidharma.

When Pu returned with the groceries, Plum Blossom did indeed prepare a sumptuous meal. She was a good cook. And Husband Pu was amazed at how silently the food had been prepared. Hitherto, the kitchen had echoed with vituperative shouts and insults directed at the hapless Ling Ling.

On this occasion, only sounds of bliss radiated from the kitchen. Wu Pu felt that a whole new era had begun on the happy day of his brother's return.

The dinner, served by Ling Ling, was a success in every way. Domestic tranquility reigned in the Wu household.

When evening fell after Hung's departure, Plum Blossom wished to make herself glamorous before retiring. Her imagination was highly erotically charged. And with every motion she made, she visualized that she was preparing to meet the attractive Captain Hung that evening for an orgy of sexual abandon.

It had never bothered Plum Blossom to allow Pu to watch her as she prepared for bed. His ogling had no effect on her whatsoever. But this evening, for a change, she was not only aware of his attention. It amused her to think of how beautifully depraved it would be if the worm were forced to watch while she and his bother frolicked in the bed.

"Watch all you want, Husband," she said contemptuously. "You are free to touch me only with your eyes. As for your ugly hands, feel free to fondle yourself at will as you gaze at my ravishing loveliness." She kneeled before her dressing table and arranged her paint and lacquer pots and her combs and brushes.

She then stood and removed her clothing as provocatively as she could, imagining Hung becoming aroused as she did so. And she was evilly tickled that she was cruelly arousing Pu's passion.

As Plum Blossom's body revealed itself to his eyes, Pu's member responded with vigor. He gazed at her perfect, inviting breasts. His lips itched to suck those nipples into granite tipped points. Without removing his gaze from his wife's performance, he slipped off his trousers and gripped his enlarged phallus with his fist.

Plum Blossom watched Pu's self-abuse with a derisive chuckle.

"That's such a disgusting reed you're grasping onto," she scoffed. "Go ahead pleasuring it. It's such a ridiculous sight to see."

Plum Blossom's scoffing did not faze Pu. As he had on previous occasions, he imagined that it was Plum Blossom's hand that grasped his manhood. And his imagination allowed him to think that his rod was as huge as he knew his brother's to be.

He increased the rhythm of his lively right hand.

As he approached his climax, Pu removed his antic hand from its pleasurable task, dropped to the floor at his wife's feet and kissed her lovely right foot. Plum Blossom spitefully kicked Pu in the face. But Pu's response to her action was close to orgasmic due to the intimacy he felt for that divine little foot that had graced his being.

His adoring look as he gazed up at her caused Plum Blossom to guffaw.

Sitting at her dressing table, she picked up a vial of Blue Dragon perfume and applied a few drops to her pubic area. She smiled, thinking of how it would meld with her own female essence to arouse Wu Hung when she had him to herself there in that very room.

At the sight of the orifice that was revealed as she did so, Pu returned to his onanism.

Plum Blossom had no interest in her husband's actions down on the floor. She returned to her toilette. She lacquered her hair, applied her cosmetics upon her lovely face and slipped into her bed.

She sprawled out, and squirmed with delight as her mind envisioned the mighty slayer of tigers lowering his lips upon her pointed nipples. Her delicate fingers, lubricated with spittle, had to substitute for his masculine lips. Her other hand slipped down to her pubis and seductively brushed the silken hairs it encountered there.

In her imagination, her middle finger became a phallus. It toyed daintily with her labia and her throbbing clitoris before entering her gift-box.

And as Plum Blossom climaxed with a mad shriek, her husband splattered his navel with his own seed, then crept over to his corner of the room, somehow pitifully satisfied.

SHATTERED DREAMS

The next day, at mid-morning, Wu Hung arrived at the house bearing all his belongings. Plum Blossom met him at the door, smiling all over. She invited him in and led him upstairs to his room.

She went to her room, changed clothes, applied makeup and returned down to the kitchen where she prepared a delicious light meal.

When Hung came back downstairs, his sister-in-law was sitting at the table. There was an assortment of appetizing snack foods and a flagon of wine on the table.

The newly donned attire she was wearing was skimpy and provocative. She was wearing a loose black silk robe with a pink chrysanthemum design on the back. The robe was cinched to her body with a white silk sash. She was wearing a pair of elegant satin slippers.

He noticed that she had applied makeup. And he detected the scent of some kind of perfume that surrounded her.

At Plum Blossom's insistence, Hung reluctantly sat down across the table from her. She poured wine into the two goblets and invited him to partake.

"I am sorry you have gone to so much trouble to prepare this meal," he told her. "I breakfasted back at the barracks this morning. The food you cooked is – I am sure – quite delicious. But I never eat unless I am hungry. That is one of the Chan Buddhist tenets I live by."

"I honor your tenets, Brother Hung," she answered. "But certainly, a bit of wine mid-morning could not possibly be offensive to your beliefs." She held up her goblet in his direction and flashed her most enchanting smile.

"It is forbidden for members of the army to partake of any alcoholic beverages during the day," he told her. "I will be returning to duty at the yamen soon and must be alert."

Plum Blossom was becoming increasingly frustrated at the way things were going. Or, to be more to the point, were *not* going. Food and wine clearly were not going to get the sexy gentleman in the mood. So, perhaps a bit of eye-candy?

Her hair was not lacquered that morning. And the clasp was positioned, purposely, quite precariously.

With a shake of her head, her beautiful long, silky tresses just happened to escape the binding and cascaded down over her shoulders. The coy smile on her face was intended to call his attention to the erotic effect the new look was intended to stimulate.

To her annoyance, Captain Hung purposefully avoided paying attention to the ploy. He was beginning to get angry at what he correctly viewed as seductive behavior on the part of his brother's wife.

Plum Blossom felt she knew men. And her experience had taught her that no man can resist temptation. The fools always, eventually, succumb.

She shrugged, causing the robe to fall from her left shoulder, completely exposing her left breast. Her triumphant smile was met by a fierce scowl.

The honorable tiger slayer rose from his seat and shook his fist at his sister-in-law. His eyes blazed in anger.

"Your actions repulse me, wife of my brother," he thundered. "I have lived my entire life honorably. Your dissolute behavior both enrages and sickens me."

Plum Blossom immediately switched roles.

"You clearly misunderstand me, Brother-in-law," she responded with cool dignity.

"The slip of my robe was inadvertent. My actions were never meant to seduce you. Much less offend you. Indeed, it is I who should be offended if you thought I had any inappropriate intentions with my husband's brother.

"I believe you owe me an apology."

Captain Hung glowered at the lying woman. And, with the dignity that seldom left him, he marched upstairs, picked up his iron club and strode back down the stairs.

Plum Blossom was terrified. She knew that the burly soldier was enraged. And she was aware that he could be merciless with that iron club he wielded. In terror, she fled into the kitchen and was pretty sure she could get out the back door into the safety of the outdoors from there.

Wu Hung's eyes did not even follow her flight. He stiffly exited the front door and marched back to the yamen, proudly carrying his iron club.

When Plum Blossom realized that the object of her affections had actually left the house, she turned around, rushed upstairs, threw herself on the bed and wept her heart out.

When Pu returned home, Plum Blossom was till distraught.

"What is the matter, Wife?" he asked. "Have you been crying?"

"Yes, you fool," she spit out. "See what you've done? You insisted that your big brute of a brother come in here and live with us. He is just a big, oversexed lummox. He came here today to move his stuff in. I prepared a nice welcoming snack for him.

"After he'd moved everything into his room, he came down here and began to take his clothes off. I protested and reminded him that he was my brother-in-law. He then suggested such vulgar and inappropriate things that I felt I had to run into the kitchen to get away from him. I was ready to flee out the back door when I realized he had put his uniform back on and had left, carrying his iron club with him.

"I have been distraught all day, fearing he would return and accost me."

Pu was astounded. He knew his brother too well to believe such charges. Yes, Hung had been gone for a long while. He had lived in the wilds and then in army camps. Even so, Pu was sure Hung could not have changed that much. But, as always, he did not contradict his wife and just let her rave on.

Later that evening, Hung returned to the house with two companions.

"I am here to get my belongings, Brother," he said calmly.

"What is the matter?" Pu asked solicitously. "You are welcome here."

"I have my reasons, My Brother," Hung answered. "It is one of Bodhidharma's precepts that a home should radiate a sense of tranquility. I leave you and my sister-in-law with compassion in my heart."

Pu stood aside as his brother and his companions marched upstairs, brought his belongings down and Hung left without any further words.

Unfortunately, Wu Hung did not leave tranquility in his wake. Plum Blossom did not give up railing at Pu about his salacious brother for nearly a week.

Two weeks later, Hung returned to Pu and Plum Blossom's house. He bore a basket containing foodstuffs and wine.

Pu invited him in and Plum Blossom was delighted to see him. The presence of the giant still filled her with surges of lust. She could not believe the feelings were not reciprocated by the imposing hunk. She smirked and felt vindicated by his return with his peace offering.

Plum Blossom had Ling Ling relieve the captain of his basket and set the offerings out on the table.

The family of three sat down together and ate and drank in harmony.

"The provincial magistrate is sending me to the imperial capital," Hung told his relatives. "To fulfill my mission, I will be away for at least two months. I am worried that during my absence, the neighborhood might not be safe for you. I have seen that there are questionable elements hanging around. So it would give me comfort, Brother, if you would curtail your absences from the house somewhat. Cut back from your peddling as much as possible.

"It would give me even more peace of mind if you would keep your doors and gates well locked. And the drapes drawn."

"If that will give you peace while you are away, My Brother," Pu agreed. "I will do as you ask."

When Pu agreed, Plum Blossom went into a fit.

"This is such foolishness, Brother-in-law," she raged. "It is insulting to your brother and to me. I will be delighted to see you go as far away as possible."

And, sobbing and shouting, she bolted from the table and ran upstairs to throw herself on the bed to weep and beat her hands against the mattress.

Plum Blossom's fury did not abate for three whole days. Pu, of course, put up with her tantrums. But he did as he had promised and cut his daily inventory in half, locked the doors and gate, and drew the curtains.

His actions were met with scoldings and abuses at first. But, as time passed, Plum Blossom cooled down and even became reconciled to the new order.

THAT PROMISCUOUS MASTER HSI

Plum Blossom enjoyed sitting on the porch and watching the world go by. But, she not only wanted to observe the passing crowd. She wanted to be seen as well. So, before going out to display herself to the world, she made herself up and dressed in her most seductive finery.

One particularly fine day, after Wu Pu had left the house with his wares she went outside to sit beneath the bamboo awning that covered the front porch.

She was adjusting one of the support-poles before taking her seat, and the pole slipped out of her hand, grazing the head of a passer-by. She threw an admiring glance at the victim of the mishap.

The man was a handsome sophisticate who was in his mid-thirties. He wore a green silk tunic and a fashionable hat whose tassels tinkled as he walked. His golden girdle was studded with jade. And he carried a gold-speckled Sichuan fan.

In short, he was the answer to a romantically inclined lady's heart.

When the attractive gentleman felt the pole hit him, his initial response was anger. But when he saw the attractive young lady appraising him, his response morphed into something quite different.

The attractive lady who was retrieving the errant pole was smiling at him seductively and measuring him attentively from his tasseled hat to his elegant thin-soled shoes.

The lovely feminine figure he took in with his eyes had an abundant, lacquered crown of blue-black hair atop a snowy white delicate face. Her eyebrows curved in delicate crescents above her almond-shaped eyes. Her lips, cherry-red, had a seductive pout. Her nose was fine and her rounded cheeks were pink. Her slender figure, prominent at the bust, was narrow at the waist. And the gentleman noted again the ample bosom and the thin, adorable feet.

Plum Blossom attempted to apologize for the accident. But the gentleman would have none of it. As the passerby skillfully attempted to explain that the accident was entirely his fault for being in the wrong place at the wrong time, Plum Blossom was keenly aware that his eyes were devouring her and happily spoke of dalliance and lust.

Next door to the Wus' house stood Mother Wong's teahouse.

Rather than continuing on his way, the gentleman turned about and entered the teahouse. Mother Wong, who had observed the entire episode at her neighbor's porch, directed her elegant customer to the roof garden of her establishment.

The gentleman in question was a dissolute dandy and playboy by the name of Hsi Men. He was a wealthy and well-connected herbalist. And Mother Wong was well aware of her customer's notoriety and wealth. He ordered tea and tea cakes.

When Mother Wong returned with the tea and cakes, she teasingly said, "I observed the catastrophic accident next door, Master Hsi. I gather that our present interests go beyond mere tea and cakes."

"You are very perceptive, dear lady," Hsi Men replied. "I feel a vital need to know about the charming bird that chirps on the porch next door. To whom is she married?"

"Would you not like to partake of a bowl of my delicious broth while we discuss the matter?" Mother Wong asked.

Master Hsi was aware that the proprietress was entering upon a business transaction with him. He was not unaccustomed to paying for valuable information and duly ordered a bowl of broth.

When Mother Wong brought the broth, it was clear to both of them where the subsequent conversation would lead.

"Now, Master," the good dame said, "I assume that you have romance on our mind."

"You are very perceptive," her customer replied with a smile.

"First," the proprietress of the tearoom continued, "allow me to answer your previous question. My neighbor, the husband of the lovely Plum Blossom who caught your eye, is none other than the pie man, Wu Pu."

"The ugly dwarf who peddles his buns, pies and tarts throughout town?" Hsi responded aghast. "The lovely lady deserves so much better than that wretch."

"You believe she needs a more worthy companion. Perhaps she would relish a love affair?" the crone suggested in her insinuating way. "Love affairs are no simple matter," she informed him. "You are talking about illicit love. For such a romance to take place, six things are required."

"And what may they be, wise lady?" Hsi Men asked, getting the drift of where the lady was leading.

Mother Wong began her discourse.

"The wooer must be physically attractive, rich, young, leisured, gentle and well-hung."

"I hope you will not find me immodest, Mother Wong," Hsi Men responded. "But I must say I believe I qualify outstandingly on all six counts. The ladies I have encountered in my amatory life have all swooned over my handsome features. I am one of the wealthiest gentlemen in the province. I am in the prime years of my youth. My time is my own and I joyfully dally the hours away. I am never abusive with members of the fair sex, but yield to their merest whims. And, as to your sixth point, I am hung like a stallion and my member has never failed to give abundant pleasure."

"That is all very well, Master Hsi," Mother Wong informed him.

"Yet, even all those features lack one essential to winning the hearts of lovelorn maidens. Particularly those who are both beautiful and romantically inclined."

"What feature are you referring to, Mother Wong?"

"Lack of generosity is the great fault in a would-be lover, Master Hsi," the business lady told him. "The man who is tight with his money will seldom find entrance into the garden of delight he seeks."

"You refer to the paradise that awaits the pilgrim that is to be found between the legs of the desired one?" the dandy suggested.

"You make me blush," the tearoom proprietor exclaimed.

Both Master Hsi and Mother Wong laughed heartily.

"You need not fear that I might be ungenerous," he told his fellow schemer. "Ten pieces of silver will be yours if my good pilgrim finds himself luxuriating in the garden."

"Then return to my shop three afternoons hence with silver in your purse," the old lady told him. "You will find the object of your affection sitting here with me, sipping tea and sewing."

Master Hsi left the teahouse wearing a lubricious smile.

Three days later, Hsi Men strolled into Mother Wong's Teahouse. He ordered tea and cakes from the waitress. In response to his question, she told him Mother Wong was upstairs in the roof garden.

When he had climbed the stairs, he called out, "Mother Wong. I've come to pay you a visit. I have asked the waitress to bring my tea and cakes up here. Is that all right?"

Mother Wong and Plum Blossom were seated at a table, sewing, gossiping and sipping tea. Mother Wong looked up and saw Hsi standing at the head of the stairs decked out in his elegant clothes, his Sichuan fan in hand. She knew for certain that he had at least five pieces of silver in his purse.

Mother Wong placed her sewing on the table, rose and went to greet the visitor.

"A delight to see you, Master Hsi," she said.

She took him by the sleeve and guided him to the table.

"This is my neighbor and good friend Plum Blossom," she told him. "She often comes here to join me to sew together. Plum Blossom, may I present Master Hsi Men?"

Plum Blossom coyly lifted her eyes, nodded, and then modestly lowered her head and proceeded with her sewing. Master Hsi was entranced at Plum Blossom's beauty. Her delicate face was crowned with a luxuriant pile of lacquered blue-back hair. Her white lawn chemise was covered by a peach-colored silk petticoat. Her trousers were of blue satin.

Hsi bowed deeply before her.

"It is an honor to meet you, fair lady," he said gently.

"The honor is mine," she replied, setting her sewing down and looking wistfully into his eyes.

Master Hsi asked Mother Wong, "Might I know the family name of your delightful neighbor?"

Just then, the waitress entered the roof garden with Men's order and placed it on the table.

"Kindly take your seat," the proprietress invited her patron.

When he had done so, she told him, "Do have a sip of tea and we'll see if you can guess who the lady is.

"Do you recall, a few days ago, an awning pole grazed your head nearby?"

"Oh, I recall it well," Hsi Men replied. "I have wondered whose home that was where the incident occurred."

There was no doubt in his mind who the gorgeous woman was who stood on that porch on that occasion. But, he knew the rules of the game and was playing it with distinction.

"The house belongs to Wu Pu, the pie man," Mother Wong informed him. "And this is his honorable wife."

"Ah, so I see now," Men replied as if surprised. "I should have recognized you immediately. You must excuse me, dear lady."

"I so regret my clumsiness on that occasion," Plum Blossom said modestly. "I hope you have forgiven me."

"There is nothing to forgive. I was simply in the wrong place at the wrong time."

Mother Wong asked Plum Blossom, "Are you acquainted with this gentleman?"

"I have not had the honor."

"The gentleman is the honorable Hsi Men, a man of high standing and wealth," the crone informed her. "He is a close friend of the Imperial Provincial Magistrate. He is known to be the richest man in the province. The large herb and pill dispensary located near the yamen belongs to him. His rice fields are the greatest in the region."

Mother Wong went on to explain how rich and famous her guest was.

Plum Blossom continued to sew and sip as she listened. The more she listened, the more interested she became in the handsome gentleman. And her interest was quite large already.

Hsi Men had an educated eye. He saw the young lady's interest increase as she listened to his importance being described.

He was quite sure now that he would be able to bed her. And soon. But he had to bide his time as Mother Wong further laid out the groundwork.

At last, the time arrived for Mother Wong to make the next suggestion.

"Master Hsi," she said. "In honor of the lovely honorable lady, perhaps you would like to order some wine." Hsi Men feigned surprise at such a novel suggestion.

"A splendid idea," he replied. "What wine do you have in the shop?"

"We have only a modest wine at the moment. The wine merchant on the other side of town has a very fine Red Dragon tiger bone wine that I usually have available, though. Lamentably we are temporarily out of it."

Plum Blossom made a feeble show of protest at the idea of anything like wine. Her protest was, of course, overlooked.

"I would like to toast the young lady," Hsi Men told his hostess. "Perhaps you can have the waitress bring up a bottle of your house wine for a start. Then, could you possibly procure a bottle of the tiger bone wine from the merchant?"

Mother Wong assured him that his request was quite possible to fulfill, and called down to the waitress to bring up a bottle of wine and two wine cups.

The wine and the cups arrived practically immediately. Mother Wong filled the cups with the wine.

Men took a silver piece from his purse and handed it to the crafty woman.

"Would you be so kind as to procure the fine wine you mentioned for us?" he asked.

"I would be delighted and honored, Master Hsi," the procuress answered. "I will go get it myself. So I will be gone for a while. In the meantime," she asked Plum Blossom, "will you be so kind as to keep our guest company while I am on my errand?"

Plum Blossom agreed to be "so kind."

As Mother Wong started down the stairs, Hsi Men toasted his companion. Out of courtesy, she took a sip. Then another. And then, still another. Master Hsi accompanied her, sip for sip.

Now, he knew, the courtship was actually launched.

Plum Blossom pushed back away from the table and cast furtive appearing glances at her swain. Hsi Men gazed at her with a fixed adoring look.

"Did I hear Mother Wong correctly?" he asked. "I believe she said you are the wife of Wu Pu, the roving pie man. But that hardly seems likely."

Plum Blossom blushed and dropped her head.

"But, my dear lady," Men said, "you are the loveliest creature in our entire province. And Wu Pu is a hideous, misshapen dwarf. How unfair of providence that you should have to suffer such an outrage."

And, with that as a launching pad for his seductive speech, the glib tongued aristocrat courted her with compliments interlaced with innuendo.

In response, Plum Blossom giggled girlishly behind her hand. She blushed, hid her eyes, gave coy glances, and blinked.

Mother Wong did not usually provide a bed as part of the furnishings of the roof garden. But, when she felt the occasion warranted, that convenient article did appear. That particular afternoon, the canny fixer felt the occasion deserved it.

"I find the heat today oppressive, dear lady," Men exclaimed. "Would you mind if I take off my coat?"

Apparently Plum Blossom did not mind, so the article of clothing was promptly shed.

"Where shall I put it?" he asked, needlessly.

Plum Blossom did not answer. But she glanced at the bed and his eyes followed her lead.

Men threw the coat in the direction of the bed. But as he did so, a sleeve swept across one of the chopsticks on the table. By chance, the stick landed on the floor between Plum Blossom's feet. Oh, dear!

"Might this be your little chopstick?" the vixen asked, planting her dainty little foot atop it. Plum Blossom was taking her own next step in the flirting game.

"I doubt it," her new rich companion replied. "I have a very large chopstick."

"I do not doubt it," Plum Blossom giggled. "Why don't you pick that one off the floor, though, to make sure."

Men bent over, and pressed his hand on his prey's colorfully embroidered slipper instead of on the implement.

"Oh, Sir," Plum Blossom smiled as maidenly as she could. "I beg you, do not take liberties. I just might scream, bringing our hostess up here to scold you."

"Our hostess is deep into the town now, in search of tiger bone wine. I doubt she would hear you," her new swain assured her.

Hsi Men dropped down onto his knees, slid his hand up from her slipper onto her thigh.

"Do not be cruel, dear dove," he implored. "Take pity on your adoring swain. I am in dire pain in need of your loving attention."

"Desist," the young lady said demurely, very unconvincingly. "I am a faithful wife and am not the sort of girl you seem to believe me to be."

"I believe you to be a kind, gentle creature who cannot find it in her heart to see a fellow human die of love before her very eyes," Men replied.

He rose up onto his feet immediately, displaying a rising phallus behind his trousers that proved he had not lied to Mother Wong when he described his manhood.

He took the willing flirt in his arms and carried her bodily over to the waiting bed.

Master Hsi was a very experienced lover. With great efficiency he deftly disrobed the object of his desire. She offered no maidenly resistance whatsoever.

Plum Blossom observed with hungry eyes as Master Hsi shed his elegant clothing with aplomb.

As he ended his disrobing by removing his remaining undergarment, the towering phallus that revealed itself made the delighted young woman gasp with joy. The paltry organ of her shriveled spouse had been so laughable all those years. Here was a puzzle worthy of her own libidinous needs.

Master Hsi pulled his latest prey's supple body to his. Her lovely breasts snuggled into his chest and his manhood pressed against her pubis. With his left hand behind her head, he drew her lips to his and as his tongue entered her mouth, hers met it willingly.

The worldly gentleman laid her gently down on the bed and gazed down on the figure of the lovely Plum Blossom stretched out before him, nude. Her nipples were already extended invitingly, teasing him to lean over and lick and suck them as though he were famished. But wait. First he had to run a caressing hand from her moist kissed lips over her chin, brushing her neck lightly, trailing a path with his middle finger down into the black silken triangle that pointed inexorable down toward the garden of delight whose entrance beckoned.

Men smoothed those pubic silken filaments with tender strokes and ran a finger over those lower welcoming lips. Welcoming indeed. For they were already moistened by an entrancing scented lubricant that emitted itself from within her garden of delights.

As her lover ran his finger gently up and down her outer lower lips, Plum Blossom's hand found her experienced lover's tower and gently, ever so gently, caressed it. Fearing that she might be overly hastening her swain's climax, she let her hand slip down and softly cradle his full scrotum for a respite.

Plum Blossom was poised, ready for her lover to grace her yearning vagina with the worthy organ that rose from the golden orbs in her right hand.

But, no. Hsi Men's mouth, tongue and hands must first be gratified by exploration of that splendid bosom, that adorable buttocks, and a lingual exploration of her pubis.

Men drew a saliva line from his lover's navel up to the cleft between her breasts with his moist tongue. As he did so, Plum Blossom's dainty right hand ever so lightly massaged his testicles.

Men's mouth found a firm grasp on each of the lovely lady's nipples in turn, sucking deeply until they extended with electric tension.

Then, he paid lingual attention to her moist vaginal lips, while – with a saliva moistened finger – he entered her anus.

Plum Blossom now yearned for entrance to her garden.

Plum Blossom parted her thighs widely, welcoming. Her body was quivering with anticipation. She could wait no longer.

"Come to me," she gasped.

As Hsi mounted her, his finger remained ensconced in her rear entry, that second pleasure spot which doubles the delight of the experienced practitioner.

Her vaginal muscles squeezed his throbbing manhood and sucked it deep into her womb.

Their mutual delight was inexpressible. The rich Chinese language has never found a word sufficient to express such unworldly ecstasy.

Men's lips met hers and she sucked his tongue ferociously.

His thighs pounded at hers with increasing momentum.

Plum Blossom's pointed fingernails scratched into her lover's back. Her fists pounded his shoulders.

Their joint passions rode higher and higher until his final lunge sent his molten discharge to a wild conclusion. Plum Blossom's own cataclysmic orgasm exceeded even his.

Hsi Men collapsed into his lover's arms. She gently ruffled his hair with her delicate fingers as their heavy breathing subsided. In time, Men's weapon rose again to its appointed task, and the lovely battle was again willingly launched.

And, with time, a third engagement of their love-match terminated.

The couple were lying, nude, in each other's arms when Mother Wong burst into the roof garden with a bottle of precious wine in hand.

She was shocked! Shocked!

She berated Plum Blossom.

"You naughty, naughty girl," she scolded. "I invited you to come here to my teahouse to sew, not to act like a hussy. I'm of a good mind to go right next door and tell your husband what you have done here in the sanctity of my shop.

The crone turned as if to go directly to see Wu Pu.

Plum Blossom called out to her.

"Oh, Mother Wong. No, no. Have pity on me."

Mother Wong turned back and faced her.

"Your plea has touched my heart," the old matchmaker said with deep compassion. "I will relent on one condition."

"Name it," Plum Blossom pleaded.

"I will keep my peace on this one condition. Henceforth, you must meet Master Hsi secretly whenever and wherever he wishes. When I call to you, you will come."

Plum Blossom readily promised.

She left the teashop and returned home, deeply satisfied.

Hsi Men remained behind.

Mother Wong asked her customer whether his experience was worth the agreed upon cost.

"Words cannot describe it," Master Men told her. "I will return tomorrow with ten pieces of silver."

They both laughed.

A NICE CUP OF ARSENIC TEA

Hsi Men arrived at Mother Wong's the next morning with money in his purse. Mother Wong was very fond of money. And the ten pieces of silver the distinguished gentleman dropped into her hands, one at a time, made her eyes twinkle and her smile muscles go into ecstasies.

The reprobate had arrived early in the morning, before the itinerant pie man neighbor usually set out on his business. But, in gratitude for her patron's prompt and generous payment, she offered to arrange for her beautiful neighbor to comply with her new obligations without much delay. She was a businesswoman and was accustomed to practice delivery on payment.

So the cunning procurer headed right out for the house next door on the pretext of borrowing a ladle.

Plum Blossom was serving her husband his breakfast when she heard a knock on the back door. When she went to answer, she was pleased to see Mother Wong there. It was clear that something was up.

"Please excuse me, Madame Wu," the visitor said. "But, I have somehow misplaced my gourd ladle. Might you be able to lend me yours for a short time?"

Plum Blossom, wondering what all this might be about, ran to the kitchen, found a ladle and brought it to the back door and gave it to Mother Wong.

"Would you care to come in?" she invited.

"No, I cannot stay," the neighbor lady replied. "There is no one minding the shop so I have to return immediately."

She gave Plum Blossom a meaningful pinch on the arm. The two had worked out that signal to let her know when Hsi Men would be waiting for her at the teahouse.

Plum Blossom rushed her husband through breakfast and sent him on his way so she could get up to the bedroom and adorn herself for her tryst.

When she arrived at the roof garden, Hsi was entranced. His paramour seemed even lovelier to him than when he had seen her the previous day. Everything about her was radiant, exciting and enticing.

Mother Wong left the bottle of fine tiger bone wine on their table. And, of course, the bed remained in the room for their disposal.

As they sipped the wine out of the same goblet, Hsi gently slipped Plum Blossom's robe up, revealing first her delicate titillating feet. The sight caused his heart to palpitate and Plum Blossom felt tingles coursing through her body as her lover began to make his welcome moves.

And, although aroused, they began the tryst by engaging in common conversation.

She asked him his age. He told her he was thirty-five. She asked him how many wives he had. He told her he had four wives. But he assured her that none of them came close to pleasing him like she did.

When she asked him about children, he told her he had just one daughter who was engaged to be married.

Men was soon enough tired of the small talk.

"Enough of such banal chatter," he said, producing a silver herb box. He took a gob of aphrodisiac paste from the coffer, placed it on his tongue, and slipped his tongue into her mouth.

The effect on their libidos was immediate and intense. The couple practically ran to the bed, shedding their garments along the way.

From that day on, the couple met each other for amorous play on a daily basis at Mother Wong's roof garden. The proprietress restricted all her other customers to the ground floor while her special guests frolicked upstairs.

But, although the couple met in private, the tea drinkers on street level caught wind, one way and another, of what was going on upstairs.

Within two weeks, gossip circulated and hardly anyone in the neighborhood was ignorant of the juicy goings-on in the tea garden on the second story of the teahouse.

But there was one person who was not privy to the salacious talk – Wu Pu the pastry peddler.

It was one of Pu's companions, Brother Yuen, the pear peddler, who could not bear to keep the secret a secret from his cuckolded friend.

The two peddlers were enjoying a respite from their rounds at a humble winehouse they frequented, over a shared bottle of cheap wine, that the gabby pear seller spilled the perfidious beans.

Wu Pu refused to believe him at first.

But, as they consumed more and more cups of the truth-enhancing liquid, he began to ask for details.

"It is all over town that your wife has a lover. And that they meet for their fun and games in the roof garden of Mother Wong's teahouse located right next door to your place.

"It is said that the couple wait until you leave in the morning to sell your pastries. As soon as you are out of sight down the road, so they say, the couple meet. And the gossip is that the things they do up there are shocking and scandalous."

Wu Pu continued to refuse to believe his companion. But as he quaffed more of the wine he said he was game to see for himself. He could put those false rumors to rest once he figured out what to do.

Brother Yuen proposed a plan whereby Pu could check out the truth or falseness of the allegations with his own eyes.

The plan was for the two of them to go to Mother Wong's Teahouse. Little Yuan would distract Mother Wong allowing Wu Pu to run into the place, rush up the stairs and check out with his own eyes whether his wife was or was not in the roof garden with a strange man.

Little did either of these simple men realize how dangerous Little Yuan's plan could be. Little Yuan knew nothing about Hsi Men or his background. The aristocrat was not a man to be messed with.

Hsi Men was not a self-made man. His ancestors had been prominent aristocrats in the province for generations. When Men was a young man, his father sent him to the Shaolin Monastery to learn the practice of wushu. The male progeny of the family had been similarly sent there for many generations.

The family believed it behooved its men to be able to protect themselves against those who coveted their wealth. At age eighteen, the heirs of the Hsi family had been sent to Shaolin for a full year of prayer, meditation discipline and wushu.

Wushu is the martial art that teaches moves that direct the practitioner to direct his inborn qi against wicked aggressors. Alas, humble men like Brother Yuan and Wu Pu knew nothing of such matters.

The monastery was founded by Bodhidharma centuries before Hsi Men was born to teach the path to a moral life through propagation the Buddhist faith, sitting meditation and, additionally through instilling the art of wushu, the means of protecting oneself from physical harm.

Hsi Men became quite proficient in wushu during his year stay in the Shaolin Monastery. However, he had no use for meditation or what he considered to be moral hogwash.

When the two street merchants had consumed enough wine to bolster their ignorant courage, they proceeded to the celebrated teahouse to put Little Yuen's plan into action. As planned, when they arrive outside the teahouse, Wu Pu hid himself behind the peony tree that grew close to the teahouse main door.

Brother Yuan strode up to the door, carrying his pear basket in hand. When he stood there brazenly, he attracted Mother Wong's attention. When she came to the door, he began berating her, saying she was a witch, a bitch and a whore.

As expected, Mother Wong was enraged, grabbed a broom and came at Brother Yuan with fire in her eyes.

When she came running after him, Yuan turned tail and headed down the street. Mother Wong was in deadly pursuit, with fire in her eyes and waving her broom in the air.

When he was at a safe distance away, Brother Yuan cast his basket aside. That was the signal for Pu to leave his hiding place and storm the unguarded teahouse. Wu Pu raced through the door and up the stairs to check for himself whether his companion's allegations were true of false.

When Pu burst into the room, Hsi Men's carefully honed instincts responded on cue. He and his lover were nude and engaged in a very compromising activity. However, he sprang out of the bed and onto his feet and leaped before the intruder in a matter of seconds.

Wu Pu was stunned by the sudden appearance of an adversary and did not have time to observe with certainty either of the two people who were occupying the roof garden. Or what they had been doing.

With flashing speed, Men struck a lightning blow to Pu's neck with the edge of his left hand while simultaneously directing the sole of his right foot in a devastating kick directly into the pit of Pu's belly.

The discharge of qi from Hsi Men's dantien was close to lethal.

Wu Pu was knocked down the stairs to the street level salon of the teahouse. Mother Wong observed the body with horror.

Fortunately, there were no customers in the salon.

The lovers upstairs rapidly clothed themselves and ran down to the street level salon. Hsi Men escaped out the back door and disappeared up an alley while Plum Blossom stood over her husband's unconscious body wringing her hands.

Blood was trickling from Pu's mouth and his face was deathly white. Mother Wong and Plum Blossom lifted the body and carried it out the back door and over to Pu's house. They laid Pu in his bed and washed the blood off his face.

Plum Blossom regretted that he had survived and hoped the blows would soon do him in.

During the next week, Wu Pu lay unconscious in his bed. He appeared somewhere between life and death. The lovers were counting on it being death.

They met every day in the roof garden making love while, next door, Plum Blossom's husband lingered, wasting away. Hsi Men continued to keep Mother Wong provided with silver for the privilege of use of the facility.

Wu Pu was completely helpless. He could not even sit up. When Plum Blossom happened to be at home, if he asked her to help him move in any way, she ignored him. He requested her to bring him hot broth and cold water. To no avail. Plum Blossom was not about to pamper the wretch.

The wife callously put on her fancy clothes and made herself up while her husband watched helplessly. She returned to their bedroom after her trysts in high spirits and with flushed cheeks. Pu could only imagine what was going on in the teagarden next door.

Plum Blossom did not permit anyone to go near him. Not even the serving maid, Ling Ling.

Ling Ling was tempted to help her master upstairs in some way. But she did not dare. She knew Plum Blossom's punishment for such an infraction would be unpleasant in the utmost.

After the fourth week of enduring his misery, Wu Pu addressed his wife.

"It is clear to me, Wife, that you are having an affair next door in the teahouse. I now am sure that I would have caught you at it, but your lover attacked me mercilessly, at your instigation. I can now see that I am likely to die from the beating he gave me and from your lack of caring for my needs after I was assaulted.

"There is nothing I can do about that. And, frankly, I do not care whether I live or die.

"But I wonder if you have taken into consideration my brother, Hung. He will be returning from his mission before long. And, what will happen then? Think about it.

"I will make a deal with you. If you attempt to nurse me back to health with compassionate attention by providing me with substance and attending to my needs, I, in turn, will not tell Hung how you have been acting toward me. But, if you persist in your heartless ways, my brother will learn about your neglect of me and how your lover beat me with his knowledge of wushu."

Plum Blossom was taken aback at first. She did not respond immediately, but rushed next door to where Hsi Men was waiting for her. She told him about the ultimatum her husband had presented her with.

Men called Mother Wong up to the roof garden to present the present dilemma to her.

"Wu Pu's mighty brother, the Tiger-slayer of King Yang Mountain will be returning to town one of these days soon," he explained to her. "I had not taken that into account. The captain could certainly, at the very least, put an end to my affair with my lover if he returns. I am now deeply in love with Plum Blossom and cannot give her up.

"I cannot think what to do. I know you to be resourceful. And I will be generous if you can solve our dilemma."

Mother Wong was, indeed, resourceful. And her resourcefulness was always greatly stimulated when she smelled silver in the offing. So the solution popped into her head immediately.

"How many pieces of silver might accrue to me if I solve your problem, Master Hsi?"

Hsi offered her five pieces of silver. Mother Wong bit her lip.

He then offered her ten pieces. She bit her lip even harder.

"All right, then," Master Hsi said in desperation. "I must have Plum Blossom as my lover. The tiger-slayer is likely to disrupt my romance. Would twelve pieces help you come up with a solution to my problem?"

"You are quite generous, Master," the old lady smiled. "For twelve pieces of silver I will give you the solution to your problem. But it can only be solved if you are willing to take Plum Blossom as your Number Five Wife. But that is impossible, of course, as long as Wu Pu lives. His end must be expedited before the tiger-slayer returns.

"If you are married before the brother gets here, your problem will be solved.

"You certainly must have arsenic in your shop, Master. Don't you?"

"Of course."

"A bit of it in the medicinal herb tea Plum Blossom will prepare to ease her husband's pain will finish the poor fellow right off. He will be duly cremated, so that no trace of the substance will be found. So when the traveling brother returns, there will be no question that the dwarf's death was in any way unusual. You will, of course, have to wait the required half-year for the legal period of the widow's mourning. But, once that mourning period has passed, you can get married. And your desire will be fulfilled. You will be legally mated to each other for eternity. And no one will question the legitimacy of your conjugal relationship."

Hsi Men was delighted with Mother Wong's solution to his problem. And he promised that he would deliver twelve pieces of silver to her after his marriage to his beloved was consummated.

He hurried to his shop immediately and returned with the medicinal herbs prescribed for invigorating the feeble and for alleviating stomach distress. And in addition, he brought along the solid dose of arsenic that was required for Plum Blossom to do the deed.

Mother Wong taught Plum Blossom how to brew the concoction.

Hsi Men brought enough of the herbs so there would be a good quantity left over in the house to demonstrate that Plum Blossom had been taking compassionate care of her husband up to the point of his demise.

"Go tell your husband you are sorry if he thought you did not care for him," Mother Wong advised her compassionate neighbor.

"Show him the herbs and tell him you went to the herbalist and got good medicine for him. When you bring the arsenic laced brew to him, urge him to drink deeply. When the arsenic begins to kick in, he will develop a fever. Then, after a while, he will lose control of his bowels and will begin moaning and shouting from the pain. Have a gag ready to keep anyone from hearing him.

"Next, he will go into convulsions. Hold him down firmly.

"The next thing that will happen, he will bleed from all seven orifices. Be sure to have hot water and cloths ready to clear away all the blood as soon as he dies. Then, once he's in his coffin and cremated, you will be rid of him and all traces of the poisoning will have disappeared. Then, you can truly prepare to be Master Hsi's wife and lover forevermore.

"Now, Plum Blossom," she continued. "Go home immediately and take care of that dear husband of yours."

"Oh, I'll take care of him all right," the young woman said. "Just see if I don't."

All three laughed heartily.

As they parted, Hsi told the two women he would return the next day at the hour of the fifth drum beat.

When Plum Blossom got home with her packages, she left the herbs and poison in the kitchen and then hurried upstairs to the bedroom. When she got there, she managed to feign tears.

She sat on the edge of the bed.

"Why are you crying?" Wu Pu asked.

"I am so ashamed," Plum Blossom replied. "I strayed from the path of righteousness, snared by an evil cad. I had already repented and had decided to confess my wayward ways to you. I had even gone to tell the scoundrel I would never see him again. That was the moment that you arrived at the teahouse to rescue me. And the villain hit and kicked you and now you are in pain. I cannot stand it.

"I went to the herbalist and bought medicinal herbs for you to give you back your strength and to relieve your internal pains. But I have not brewed them yet for fear you wouldn't trust me and would not take the medicinal tea."

"I trust you now," Pu told her. "And I will blot the whole unfortunate matter from my memory as you nurse me back to health. I will not breathe a word about the unfortunate incident when Hung returns.

"Please brew up the health-giving herbs now. I can hardly wait to get better."

Plum Blossom went down to the kitchen and prepared the health-giving tea. And, of course, she stealthily added the death-giving poison.

She brought the concoction up to the bedroom and assisted her husband to sit up. Then she spooned some of the broth-like mixture into her husband's trusting mouth.

Wu Pu made a sour face.

"That is the worst tasting thing I have ever sipped," he complained.

"Yes," Plum Blossom answered. "The herbalist told me that it would be hard for you to get down. But that the important thing is that it will revive and heal you. Come now. Take your medicine so you can get well soon."

She got Pu to sip from the cup until he had drunk every bit of the foul tasting liquid.

As soon as he had finished drinking it, Pu's face screwed up with pain.

"Oh, Plum Blossom," he cried out. "I feel such pain in my stomach."

"I was told that there would be temporary discomfort," his wife told him. "It will soon ago away. And you will be feeling much better in a few moments."

Pu began to moan. And Plum Blossom knew he would begin to scream soon if she did not act quickly.

So, she took the pillow from behind his head, placed it over his face and sat down on top of it.

She could hear his muffled shrieks and feel his wrenching below her on her bottom. But she remained atop him resolutely until she felt him expire.

With relief that the task was done, Plum Blossom got off the bed and placed the pillow back underneath her husband's head.

Just as she sighed her relief that the gruesome task was over, she heard a knocking on her back door.

She went downstairs and let Mother Wong in.

"Is it done?" the beldam asked.

"Yes," the young widow told her. "It is finished."

"Did you clean the blood seepage off him?" Mother Wong asked.

When Plum Blossom apologized that she had not had time to clean her husband up, the older woman proceeded directly to the kitchen and began boiling some water. When the water was hot enough, she put a washcloth in the pail and led Plum Blossom up to the bedroom.

Mother Wong pulled the covers off Wu Pu's corpse and then removed his nightclothes. With her washcloth, she washed away the blood that had oozed from his seven orifices. Then she and Plum Blossom dressed the body in Pu's finest clothes, including his hat, shoes and hose. They went downstairs and got a table from the kitchen and hauled it into the front room. Then they went back up, hauled him down, and laid the corpse out on the table. They veiled his face with crepe and covered his body with a blanket.

Now that the hardest part was done and over with, Mother Wong went back home.

Following custom and propriety, Plum Blossom remained seated next to the body all night long. However, with not so much as a tear in her eye. And certainly with no feelings of remorse.

At the hour of the fifth drumbeat, Mother Wong and Hsi Men came to the house as though to pay their respects to the dear departed.

Plum Blossom asked Hsi Men what he was going to do now to keep her safe from the law.

"Don't you worry your pretty little head about that, my dear," he told her.

"I have a very good relationship with Hu Kiu, the provincial coroner. He will take care of everything.

So Plum Blossom was sure she had nothing to worry about. That after her period of mourning, a whole beautiful life awaited her.

THE SEVENFOLD ROADS
TO BLISS

Mother Wong went out to purchase the things necessary for Wu Pu's funeral. She bought a coffin, some incense, candles and silver slippers. She returned to Wu's front room; she placed a lamp at the corpse's head and lit it.

Soon the neighbors began to arrive to view the corpse. The young widow sat at the side, hiding her face in feigned grief.

When nosy neighbors asked her what Pu had died of, she sobbed and told them "stomach cramps."

"My dear husband was in pain. I brought him herbal medicines that eased the pain somewhat, but unfortunately they did not manage to cure the disease. Just at the hour of the third drumbeat, the dear man passed away. Oh, how I shall miss my dear, beloved husband."

The recitation was sometimes followed with sobs, but never with tears.

The visitors, of course, drew their own conclusions. But, they uttered the traditional words of solace and left the widow to her pantomime.

Somewhat before noon, Hu Kiu was heading for the house of mourning to fulfill his function. Hsi Men encountered him on the road. He greeted his friend with a wide smile.

"I see you are on your way to the home of the deceased pie man to make your official findings prior to Wu Pu's cremation, Master Hu."

"Just so, Master Hsi," the coroner bowed politely.

"There is a fine little wine-shop just down this side-street, Master Hu," Hsi Men said. "Won't you favor me by being my guest for a cup?" No one ever refused a powerful person like Hsi by declining such an invitation.

"I would be honored," the coroner replied.

The two men entered the first class wine-house and proceeded up to the reserved second floor.

Hsi Men ordered a large pot of hot-spiced wine accompanied by wine cakes. It was an elegant display. Hu Kiu was impressed and was aware that his host was about to make him a proposition. He was quite certain that the offer would be well worth accepting.

The men sipped and nibbled silently, their only communication being reciprocal smiles and head bows.

After a while, Master Hsi reached into his purse and laid fifteen pieces of silver in the middle of the table. Then he broke the silence.

"My dear, good friend," he proclaimed. "You know how much I respect you and value your friendship. You would honor me by accepting this token of my affection."

Hu Kiu nodded his head respectfully and said, "I honor you as well, Master Hsi. And I am always pleased when I can find a way to be of service to you."

He picked up the money and placed it in his own purse.

"I would be most pleased, Master Hu," the host said, "if the body of Wu Pu, the pastry peddler, could remain properly covered until it has been cremated."

Hu Kiu was not about to insult a man of his host's influence by refusing an innocent request of such delicacy. Master Hsi was clearly a very compassionate man and did not wish his friend the pastry peddler's carnal remains to be subject to the possible scoffs of his neighbors.

The friends finished the wine and cakes in silence, left the wine-house and parted ways. Hsi Men went his way and Hu Kiu proceeded along his way to the house of mourning.

The two cremators were waiting for the coroner outside the house. The three men entered the house together.

The widow was waiting for them, seated beside the body of her husband.

Hu Kiu asked her, "Of what did your husband die, Madame Wu?"

"Of stomach cramps, if it please your honor," she said with a hint of a sob in her voice. "My dear husband complained of stomach distress four weeks ago. I took good care of him. I went to the herbalist who put together medicinal herbs to relieve his suffering and cure his disease. You will find the left over leaves in the kitchen still.

"The medicine did relieve some of his suffering. But, alas, the sickness was too great to be overcome by the medicine. And, oh, I shall miss the good man greatly."

"Courage, Widow Wu," the coroner said. "Your husband was known to be a good man and his soul is even now in Heaven."

Those were lines the good coroner had occasion to repeat often.

The fifteen pieces of silver in his purse and the good will of the powerful aristocrat were sufficient enough reason to prevent him from inspecting the body beneath the coverings.

The cremators' faces registered surprise that the requirement of inspection was ignored. Master Hu handed each one a piece of silver and the two men overlooked the irregularity.

The cremators placed the body in the coffin and transported it to the Cloister of Gracious Recompense where the bonzes performed of the appropriate rites over the body. The funeral pyre was lit and the coffin was set atop the blaze.

The remaining ashes were disposed of by the cremators in the city moat. There was no trace whatsoever of any kind of questionable behavior on the part of anyone.

When Plum Blossom returned to the house after the funeral, her lover was already inside to greet her. The two were ready for the fleshly pleasures that can be indulged in wantonly in both horizontal and vertical positions.

With his lover's husband dispatched, Hsi Men relished the freedom to indulge in the sevenfold roads to bliss. The furtive nature of his hitherto relations with his beloved could now be dismissed.

Hsi Men was a past master of the sevenfold roads.

Now, his skill and adeptness, matched with his lover's natural gifts and imagination, would provide a theater for a display of lovemaking fit to be witnessed by the gods.

By the time he was seventeen, Hsi Men had already become master of the dragon tail technique. Shortly thereafter, he was renowned for his mastery of the wren's tooth. And his adeptness with the butterfly claw was declared a marvel indeed by the cognoscenti.

Plum Blossom, from before her flowering, was enraptured by her own sexuality and sensuality. Her natural carnality made her an ideal consort for her new lover's expertise.

An expert at the locust leap requires a mate finely attuned to fleshly sensitivity. Plum Blossom did not need to be tutored in the subtleties of passionate inaction and passive action necessary to accomplish that sexual delight.

What a delight it was to Hsi Men that he found a partner of such perfect wantonness that she was a peer rather than a pupil.

The couple soon settled upon an exquisite routine.

On the auspicious occasion of Wu Pu's cremation, they began their festival of carnality with the Dead Warrior's Reward. It is a technique Hsi Men had never dared entrust to any of his wives or ancillary lovers. Plum Blossom, however, came by the necessary skills required naturally.

For the Dead Warrior's Reward, Men lay prone on the silken divan, garbed in his golden silk robe, and emptied his lungs of air. He held his body as rigid as a corpse in rigor mortis.

Plum Blossom crept over her lover's deathlike body gasping sobs.

In apparent agony, she tore off her own clothing and wildly undid all of her lover's buttons and hooks until his body was as unclad as her own.

She checked for signs of a pulse by pressing her sensual lips at his chest and neck. She collapsed in grief atop his prone body when she was assured that the spirit had departed his body.

She sat upright on the corpse's chest and attempted artificial respiration by pressing down on him with her ineffably gorgeous moon-shaped buttocks. She rose and sank, rhythmically. But Hsi Men's disciplined control kept even a breath of air from stirring.

His role was that of sensual passivity. And he played it superbly.

Plum Blossom reversed position on her lover's chest and bent forward so her fragrant treasure box was gazing at his face. As she bent forward, her lips approached the magnificent tower that jutted up from her lover's loins. Her tongue flicked out like that of a chameleon and darted all about the pulsing head of that minaret. As she flicked her tongue, her mouth made ardent sucking sounds.

The dead warrior's tower throbbed, but he continued to lie as still as death itself.

The widow's mouth departed from the yearning staff. Her tongue traced arabesques about the warrior's hairy scrotum. Then, leaning farther forward, she ran her slick tongue down his thighs. She straightened out, her legs stretched straight above his head, her treasure box grazing his face, and her naval pressing against his manhood. In this position, she sucked his toes, one by one, in sequence.

She then slid forward, leaving a streak of her fragrant juices across her lover's abdomen.

The grieving widow spread her lover's legs and kneeled between them, facing the abandoned phallus.

With her delicate hands, she grazed at the yearning tower and its globular appendages until a pearl-like drop emerged from the mini-slit at its summit onto her index finger.

After that perfect moment, Plum Blossom resumed her mount on Hsi Men's chest. And with her silk slippered feet, encircled the desperate rod and brought it to exquisite release.

As the tower erupted, Plum Blossom shrieked in delight that her dead warrior had been brought back to life.

Following the Dead Warrior's Reward, it was time for the happy couple to play The Sick Maiden's Return.

Plum Blossom began by clapping her hands, as tradition dictates. And the couple engaged in that entertainment with high abandon.

For the next several weeks, Hsi Men visited Plum Blossom's house surreptitiously from Mother Wong's rear entrance to the back door of Plum Blossom's home.

But, in time, he went directly from the street to the back door, usually accompanied by Tai, his little serving boy.

Many a time Men stayed with Plum Blossom three, four, or five days at a time, never leaving the house.

Those absences from home became annoying to his wives. So, to placate his household, the master began to stay away from his new lover somewhat.

After an absence of some days, Plum Blossom met Men with a bit of temper showing.

"It's only business, Sweetheart," he said, placating her. "After all, I do have business and social obligations. But today is a holiday and I've brought you some presents I bought for you at the Temple Market."

And the trinkets were quite pleasing to Plum Blossom.

Men called Little Tai who came trotting into the room toting a large bag. From the bag the lad scooped out lavish gifts onto the table. There was jewelry, pearls, carvings, silks and satins.

Plum Blossom was delighted and ordered Ling Ling to serve Men tea and cakes.

Later, Mother Fu, who could be called upon to serve as a cook when needed, prepared a dinner of chopped goose and chicken, boiled rice, fruit and vegetables. The loving couple sat thigh-by-thigh eating from the same dish and drinking from the same cup.

After dinner, Hsi Men asked Plum Blossom to play him a tune on the pipa.

He loved how she played so skillfully and sang so beautifully.

When his lover finished and laid down her instrument, Hsi Men kissed her mouth and fondled her crotch.

The couple became more passionate. Men removed one of her embroidered satin slippers, poured wine into it and drained it to the last drop.

He barred the door and led her up to the bedroom where they engaged in their repertoire of carnal delights.

Hsi Men had a well-educated tongue. He had very refined taste buds that savored the delights of excellent cuisine. It could utter delightful and enticing words that had the effect of setting a woman's vagina a-tingle. And, that tongue could explore the fragrant interiors of a girl's two mouths with finesse. He could maneuver that educated member in his mouth into quivers and flutters along his lover's clitoris and vagina.

He had a very popular tongue.

But he was not alone in possessing a titillating tongue. When Plum Blossom encircled the spongy head of her partner's organ with her sensual lips, she managed to insert the dainty tip of her moist tongue into the tiny slit that crowns the bulb at the same time that Men was doing his tongue flutter in her fragrant love box.

To add spice to the feast, each had a finger delicately ensconced deep within the brown starfish that graces the rear orifice of the body.

In due time, Plum Blossom felt the slit which her tongue was servicing expand. And as his creamy masculine elixir spurted into her hungry mouth, her love-purse spasmed and clenched his probing tongue.

The couple yelled out in wild ecstasy and collapsed into a riot of laughter.

They soon revived and engaged in both spontaneous erotic activities or revived one or more of the sevenfold roads of sensual delight they were so good at.

While the couple thus disported themselves, Mother Fu, Little Tai and Ling Ling were in the kitchen washing dishes and pots and pans.

Finally, after Hsi Men and Plum Blossom had exhausted their capacity to frolic, Men decided to leave.

And, leaving some coins for his mistress, he put on his mask and left, trailed by his tiny servant.

THE OVEN DOOR IS OPEN

Following that happy reconciliation, Hsi Men stayed away from Plum Blossom for a month. During that time, Number Three Wife had died and he had married a thirty-year-old widow to take her place.

And he also promoted his maidservant to the rank of Number Four Wife.

During that month, Plum Blossom stood on the porch much of the day, leaning on the doorpost, waiting for her lover to return.

Several times she sent Mother Wong to Hsi Men's home, but the gatekeeper did not allow her on the property. Plum Blossom even sent Little Ying Ying to inquire about Men's absence. Ying Ying was too bashful to even approach the gatekeeper, and, like Mother Wong, she returned home without news of Master Hsi. But Plum Blossom punished her maid severely anyway, each time she came back without news of the missing lover.

On the day before Hsi Men's birthday, Plum Blossom felt desperate. She felt she had to see her lover. So she sent once more for Mother Wong. There certainly had to be a way to get the crone to bring Men to her.

When the avaricious old lady arrived, Plum Blossom removed a valuable gold and silver clamp from her hair. She knew that Mother Wong would find a way to perform the task if the reward was great enough. The clasp was worth enough to motivate the procuress.

"Kindly bring Hsi Men here to me, Mother Wong," Pear Blossom pleaded.

Mother Wong appraised the value of the hair clamp and smiled her wry smile.

"It shall be done," she replied.

Mother Wong knew where to look to find the rakehell.

In a neighborhood not far from the yamen was a quarter called The Flower Garden District where houses of joy abounded. In the early hours of the morning, when the frequenters of the joy houses started heading on their way back home, Mother Wong loitered around and paid attention to what was happening.

And, sure enough, it was not long before she spied her quarry leaving a particularly notorious joy house, dead drunk. He was being helped up onto his saddle by a couple of servants when she caught sight of him. The roué was wobbling dangerously when she approached him.

She stepped up to his horse and took hold of the bridle.

"Well met, Master Hsi," she greeted him.

"Ah, ha!" the tipsy master replied. "As I live and breathe. It is the good Mother Wong. Has my little dove sent you out to search for me?"

"She misses you, Master," Mother Wong replied.

"Yes, yes. So I have been told," Men slurred. "And I, in turn, miss her. Let us proceed and visit the little darling."

Keeping her hand firmly on the bridle, Mother Wong led the stallion towards Plum Blossom's home.

As they approached, Mother Wong rushed ahead and informed the young widow that her lover was approaching at that early hour.

Plum Blossom quickly got dressed, made herself up and went out onto the porch to await him. Her heart fluttered when she saw his approach atop his horse.

When he arrived, Hsi Men was still quite drunk and needed the help of his two servant boys to dismount. When his feet were safely on the ground, he hung onto Mother Wong's shoulder and staggered forward to embrace his lover.

Although Plum Blossom was delighted to see him, she could not help but greet him with a snide reproach.

"Nice you finally managed to drop by," she said sarcastically. "Even if you had to be dragged here by your horses bridle. I hope your new girlfriend has lots of patience. She'll need it."

"Come, come," Men answered. "You jump to conclusions my dear. There is no new girlfriend. You remain my only love.

"I have been extremely busy. And not only with my business dealings. But also, I've been overwhelmed with all the arrangements I'm involved in for my daughter's wedding. You cannot imagine the time such preparations take."

Plum Blossom did not quite believe him. But she did not wish to lose him, either. So she managed to curb her anger.

When she invited her lover inside, Mother Wong decided it was time to take her leave and return to her teahouse.

When Hsi Men and Plum Blossom entered the house, obedient Little Ying Ying entered the room bearing tea bowls and a pot of jasmine tea.

While Ying Ying set up the table, Plum Blossom ran off to fetch the presents she had been collecting as gifts for Men's birthday.

Among the presents was a pair of black satin slippers, a rose petal sachet, bamboo knee guards, a pastel silk girdle, a pink sash and a broad hairpin decorated with a jade plum blossom design.

Hsi Men wrapped his arms about her sloppily and kissed her deeply.

He picked her straightway up in his arms, carried her upstairs to the bedroom and pitched mad woo at her all day and all night long.

The next morning, before the lovers awakened, a messenger in a military uniform arrived at the door bearing a letter from Wu Hung.

Mother Wong was already up at the time and spotted the messenger. She went out and inquired what he wanted.

"I have a message from Captain Wu Hung for his brother Wu Pu," he told the old lady.

"Wu Pu and his whole family are at the cemetery. Leave the letter with me and I will see that it gets delivered when they all return," Mother Wong lied.

The messenger gave her the letter, saluted and left.

Mother Wong rushed to Plum Blossom's door and knocked furiously.

When Plum Blossom came down and opened the door, Mother Wong told her breathlessly, "Look! A messenger just came with this letter from Wu Hung. I read it while you were coming downstairs. It says he'll be coming here soon. We have to get busy and take action."

Hsi Men was coming down the stairs and heard the news.

"When will he get here?" he asked.

"Around the middle month of autumn," Plum Blossom told him as she scanned the letter. "What should we do now?"

It was Mother Wong who, as usual, came up with a suggestion.

"My advice is this," she said. "The half year of mourning for Wu Pu's death is coming to an end now. What you need to do is go contact a couple of bonzes to perform the burning of the soul-tablet. Once that ceremony is completed, they can marry you. And once you two are married and living together, you will be united for the rest of your lives and you will be safe. And you can count on me to know what to do about the captain once he gets here."

Hsi Men agreed with Mother Wong's analysis and the three plotters sat down to a breakfast served by Little Ying Ying.

The half year of mourning for Wu Pu's death finally came to an end. Hsi Men brought six pieces of silver to Widow Plum Blossom to give to the bonzes. Six bonzes from the Cloister of Gracious Recompense consequently came to her house to perform the daylong rites for Wu Pu's soul and for the burning of the soul-tablet.

While the bonzes were making preparations downstairs, Hsi Men and Plum Blossom were quietly cavorting upstairs in the bedroom.

The service began downstairs with the beating of drums, the ringing of bells and he chanting of invocations before the statue of Buddha. Simultaneously, upstairs, Plum Blossom was beating a hearty tattoo with Hsi Men's drumstick.

At noon, Plum Blossom's presence was required below as chief mourner. She made herself up, lacquered her hair, put on her mourning robe and walked gracefully downstairs.

She walked to the altar and kowtowed to the idol of Buddha.

When the bonzes got an eyeful of the gorgeous mourner, all Hell broke loose. Their manhoods tented onto their monk robes and lust crazed their eyes.

The abbot himself, made mad by lust, forgot the necessary invocation. Instead of the sutras, he babbled garbage. The monk in charge of the censor swung it wildly and knocked over a flowerpot. A third monk, instead of reciting prayers, raved on about the beauties of the widow's breasts and buttocks. One of the drummers beat another brother's head with his drumstick. The cymbals were beaten against the altar. It was a regular riot.

While havoc reigned in the front room, Widow Plum Blossom retired to her chambers to pay her special reverences to her swain's member. She had stashed away sufficient portions of the wine and garlic seasoned meat that had been procured for the ritual feast to accommodate her private upstairs party.

Downstairs, the monkish revelers raided the kitchen and added gluttony to their madcap antics.

During the upstairs reveling, it occurred to Hsi Men to perch a pinch of garlic atop his private tower. Plum Blossom pecked it off with her lips like a hungry sparrow. Her lover continued to replace the morsels one by one and the little sparrow engaged her puckish mouth by nibbling them right off.

She poured wine over her lover's belly and thighs and licked off every drop. Hsi Men, in turn, poured wine over her breasts, her navel and her bush. Nor was much liquid spilled, for this tongue and lips devoured every drop.

One of the bonzes with acute ears heard the giggles and laughter that emitted from the boudoir upstairs.

He staggered up and put his ear to the door.

He heard the widow's voice urging, "Harder, darling. Pump ever harder. More! More! The oven door is open and must roast the sacred sausage soon!"

The bonze was mightily amused and led his brothers up the stairs to enjoy listening to the couple's orgy in the boudoir.

In an ecstasy of passion, their phalli pressed up against their robes as they danced down the stairs holding hands and laughing.

They dropped hands when they reached the front room again, and before the statue of the Buddha some practiced self-abuse while others found partners in sodomy.

When all six bonzes had climaxed, they dropped to the floor exhausted.

Mother Wong was curious about the noises she had heard inside her neighbor's house. She stepped inside and was amazed at what she saw.

"Is the service over?" She asked archly.

"The oven door is open and must roast the sacred sausage soon," the abbot giggled in response.

At that point, Hsi Men, dressed in his robe and carrying his purse, came down the steps.

He laughed at the allusion and doubled the fee for the requiem services.

The abbot said he would love to express his gratitude to the widow upstairs.

Hsi Men thanked him but told him the widow gratefully declined.

And that is how the death rites of Wu Pu were celebrated.

HOLY MATRIMONY

The day after the requiem rites were celebrated, Hsi Men sent servants to Plum Blossom's house to pack up all her belongings. And the following day, the eighth day of the eighth month, he married her and had her things transported to his own properties. And, he sent a litter to transport her elegantly, in style, to her new home.

He installed her in a lovely pavilion that he re-named Plumtree House in a sequestered corner of his park. The pavilion was exquisitely furnished, with special attention given to a large black lacquered bed.

Plum Blossom was ranked Number Five Wife, since Hsi Men had married two ladies since he had met Plum Blossom.

Moon Lady, Number One Wife, previously had two maids, Rosebud and Jade Flute. Hsi Men transferred Rosebud to attend on Plum Blossom. Rosebud was instructed to call the new wife "Madame."

The day after her arrival, Plum Blossom attended carefully to her toilette, dressed in her finest apparel and paid her respects to Moon Lady and the other wives.

As Plum Blossom entered the room of Number One Wife, Moon Lady, made a quick educated appraisal. She saw that the new wife was quite lovely, exuded sexuality, and had the power to drive men mad. She thought Plum Blossom a good addition to the household.

Once in the room, Plum Blossom dropped to her knees before Moon Lady and kowtowed four times.

Moon Lady, by custom, presented the new wife with the traditional welcoming slippers.

The other wives were in the room and Plum Blossom greeted them, in order of rank: Sunflower, Jade Fountain and Snow Blossom.

Moon Lady ordered a chair to be bought in for Plum Blossom and then called all the maids into the room. She informed all the servants that Plum Blossom was to be honored as their "Fifth Mistress" and was to be addressed as "Madame."

Seated in her chair, Plum Blossom now was able to steal stealthy glances at her fellow wives.

First, she appraised Moon Lady. She pegged her at twenty-seven years of age. Moon Lady's complexion was smooth and ivory white. Her eyes were round and soft appearing, like newly picked apricots. Her movements were supple and dignified. And her speech patterns were cultivated.

Plum Blossom knew that Number Two Wife, Sunflower, had been a singing girl in a house of joy when Hsi Men encountered her. She was inclined towards plumpness. What men referred to as pleasingly plump. She had inhabited the demimonde with refinement and had a dignified air about her.

Plum Blossom estimated the age of Jade Fountain, Number Three Wife, as thirty-five. She was full-figured and beguiling. Her round face was freckled, but charmingly. Pear Blossom saw with a frown that Jade Fountain's feet were as tiny as her own.

Plum Blossom had already learned that Number Four Wife, Snowblossom, had been one of the servants before being wed to Men. She was petite and was an artful cock of exotic dishes. She had heard that she danced beautifully. And she appeared to be charming in a timid way.

Pear Blossom now had her four fellow wives firmly characterized in her mind.

Beginning the next morning, Plum Blossom had a definite routine going.

She awoke early and paid a visit to Moon Lady. She relieved her of such disagreeable tasks as sewing and manual work. She was more than willing to be helpful to Number One Wife. And referred to her always as "Honored Madame."

Moon Lady was pleased and positively affected by the new wife's solicitous behavior. The reaction of the other three wives was of quite another nature. They were jealous of the new arrival's sex appeal.

From the day Plum Blossom had moved in, Hsi Men did not leave the park. Plum Blossom's little maid, Rosebud, was not averse to gossiping with the other maids. And those other maids loved to share the dirt with their mistresses.

Thus, Wives Number Two, Three, and Four learned about the days and hours of sensual delight that transpired within the walls of Plumtree House.

Among Plum Blossoms special skills that got bandied about by the wives and servants was the one dealing with the tiresome pauses that Nature seems to demand after the male has spurted his love elixir and is left with a flaccid member.

How disheartening it is for the mistress of the situation to be confronted with a limp useless bit of flabby penis so soon after having felt the hearty thrusts and volcanic eruption within her love-purse.

A lover such as Plum Blossom, who has studied the arts of love since childhood, does not simply stare at the sleeping sausage in bewilderment and grief.

Even before the residue of her own emissions had dried off the apparently moribund male appendage, Plum Blossom's lips were kissing the mushroom like terminal of her stretched out lover. She slowly opened her lips and sucked the limp darling into her warm, sweet mouth. That love-muscle joyfully rested there, content in its cozy cavern.

From Rosebud's tattling, everyone was made aware of how grateful Hsi was for this respite. The painful pauses of waiting helplessly after orgasm can be dealt with by males by feigning sleep. Or by futilely grabbing their own recalcitrant members and caressing them with gentle or vigorous fists.

The only true assistants to revitalizing a limp phoenix, as Plum Blossom knew so well, were a pair of knowledgeable lips, a warm, moist mouth, and an educated tongue.

The sleepy serpent stirs, slithers farther into the comfortable cavern, and lodges cozily in the educated throat. At that point, the mistress of the bedchamber softy encloses the glans in a loving grasp with her enclosing lips to totally restore it to rise up gloriously back into its former vigorous life.

"Ah, my love," Master Men was heard to sigh, grasping her buttocks and entering his fingers into her dual orifices. "You have re-sharpened my saber."

Plum Blossom deftly sat up and settled herself expertly onto his pulsing tower and slipping it into her garden of delights with tantalizing slowness; she rode the monster up and down, in gradually in increasing tempo.

She teased him by showing erotic restraint.

As they spasmed together, he encircled her with his robust arms and pulled her towards him so her breasts embraced his chest.

Little Rosebud was expert at hiding in dark corners and observing wide-eyed. And she did not hold back in telling others what she saw. Her fellow servants certainly delighted in hearing the nitty-gritty about the happenings in the bedchamber.

Nor did those maids shrink from passing the delightful details on to their mistresses.

The already jealous wives were quite aware that the new wife proved awesome competition.

THE RETURN OF THE TIGER SLAYER

On the first third of the eighth month, Captain Wu Hung, the Tiger Slayer of King Yang Mountain, finally arrived back in the province.

The captain had, of course, received word while he was gone that his brother had died. He was fiercely determined to find out precisely, right down to the day and when his brother had died, the cause of Pu's death. And he was interested to learn what herbs and medicines had been used to treat his condition.

Captain Wu was suspicious about what had happened and intended to get to the bottom of the matter.

He went to Mother Wong as a first source of information. What she told him skirted the truth somewhat.

"Esteemed Captain," she said. "Your brother, Wu Pu, lamentably died on the twentieth day of the fourth month of severe stomach cramps.

"He was sick for eight or nine days with the disease. If you are interested in his treatment, you will still find some of the unused herbal medicines in the kitchen of his house.

"His devoted wife, Plum Blossom, was left destitute by her loss.

But, because she had nowhere to turn, after the traditional half year of mourning, a gentleman from the capital proposed to her and she married him. After the marriage, the couple left for the capital. She took everything with her except Little Ying Ying. She left the maid with me to care for until your return."

Wu Hung realized that was all he was likely to get from the old lady. So he sighed and left the teahouse dissatisfied.

Hung returned to his barracks and sent one of his men out from there to purchase mourning clothing and the sacrificial supplies appropriate to honor the ghost of his brother Wu Pu. His fellow guardsman returned with a mourning coat and fruit, sweets, incense, candles, paper images and ghost money.

Garbed in his new mourning coat, Hung went to his brother's house and set up the altar that had been used for the previous requiem.

At the tenth hour, he placed the offerings before the altar, set out a bowl of sacramental wine, arranged and raised the death flag and lit the candles and the incense.

As the smoke from the incense ascended, he called upon his brother's ghost.

"Oh, my dear Brother Pu. I feel your presence near. When you lived, you were humble and conciliatory. It is hard for me to see how you could possibly have died during my absence. If you were harmed by anyone, speak to me so I can avenge you and deal with whoever wronged you."

Wu Hung sat cross-legged in the deep meditation he practiced as a Chan Buddhist. As he did so, he felt a cold emanation emerge from the altar. A mystic aura seemed to surround him. And a voice sounded within his head.

"I have been sorely wronged."

The apparition disappeared back into the altar and the ghost-voice faded with the presence.

At that point, Wu Hung swooned and lost consciousness.

At the hour of the fifth drumbeat, Wu Hung awoke to the crowing of a cock. The incense and candles had all burned out.

His guardsmen entered the house just then and set up the front room as it had been before the obsequies.

Little Ying Ying dutifully prepared a morning broth for the men.

After the breakfast, Hung and his men thanked Ying Ying and left the house in her care.

On his way back to the barracks, Wu Hung asked the neighbors what they knew or surmised about his brother's death. And he asked them what they knew about Plum Blossom's disappearance.

The neighbors had information and suspicions galore. But they were loath to fall into disfavor with the rich and powerful Master Hsi Men. So, the most they were willing to tell him was that he might try to get information from Mother Wong, Little Yuen the pear seller and Hu Kiu the coroner.

Following their advice, the first person Hung questioned was Brother Yuen.

He spied him in the marketplace. The little fellow was buying rice and placing it in his basket. When Yuen looked up he was immediately aware of Wu Hung's presence. He went right over to the captain without being approached.

Wu Hung greeted the little pear vendor friendlily.

"How nice to see you, Little Brother Yuen," he smiled.

"Greetings, Captain," Yuen replied. "I know what you want. You want me to tell you things. But, unfortunately, you see, I can't help you. I would, of course, like to. But I cannot. I have a 60-year-old father who is dependent on me. And I can't let anything get in the way of my business."

Wu Hung placed his massive hand gently on the lad's shoulder and steered him towards a nearby tavern.

When they sat at a table, the captain ordered a fine meal.

As Brother Yuen was hungrily stuffing his mouth with the goodies and washing them down with wine, Hung said, "I see that you're a dutiful son. Master Bodhidharma teaches us that we must honor our elders.

"Your filial piety touches me. I would like to help. Here!"

With that, Wu Hung removed five pieces of broken silver and set them on the table before Brother Yuen."

"You would honor me by taking the silver pieces," he said. "For they are for the benefit of your aged father."

Brother Yuen thereupon swept up the silver and dropped it into his own purse.

"I wish I had more at this moment for your progenitor," Hung continued.

"When I am able to get justice in the case I am pursuing, I will give you ten full pieces of silver. With that amount, you will have enough to start a real business of your own.

"Now, tell me, Brother Yuen. For the sake of your venerable father, tell me who did my sister-in-law marry? What was happening that brought on my brother's death? Just simply tell me what you know."

Little Brother Yuen's tongue was somewhat loosened by wine. And he knew his father could live for the next five months on the silver he'd just slipped into his purse. So the whole messy matter of Pu's death would be over before he could be in any jeopardy.

So he told Captain Wu, in detail, about what had been going on between Plum Blossom and Hsi Men in the roof garden of the teahouse. He told him about his plan to get Pu past Mother Wong and up to where the tryst was taking place. And about Hsi Men's wushu kick to Pu's abdomen which sent him down the stairs and into a pitiful state of health from which he had apparently died.

"And where did my sister-in-law go after Wu Pu died?" Hung asked.

"Hsi Men sent a marriage litter to the house and took her away. That is the last thing I know," the pear peddler told him.

"Are you sure that everything you've told me is the absolute truth?" Hung asked.

"I will swear to every word of it if asked by the authorities."

"Thank you for your information," Hung told the peddler. He dished out one more coin to him.

"Now, tell me," he asked further. "Where I can find Hu Kiu, the coroner?"

"No one knows," Yuen told him. "Three days ago, when he found out that you had returned, he took off for somewhere. No one knows where."

Hung and Yuen finished their meal and each went on his own way.

The following morning, Wu Hung reported to the courtroom of the District Mandarin. He kowtowed before the official and cried out "Injustice!"

The Mandarin instructed him to arise and state the nature of his claim.

Wu Hung recited his charges, to wit:

That the missing coroner, Hu Kiu, had accepted bribes and had ruled falsely about the death of Wu Pu. That Mother Wong had acted as a procurer and was an accessory to murder. And that Hsi Men had committed both adultery and murder.

The news of Wu Hsi's charges was reported to Hsi Men within an hour. And he immediately sent two of his representatives to the Mandarin and his entire staff carrying large sums of money.

The next morning, Wu Hung went to the District Mandarin's courtroom to hear the official reactions.

They were read aloud by the top official himself:

"You are young and naive, Captain Wu. So, you must not pay attention to such gossip. It would not be wise for you to make an enemy of as powerful man as Hsi Men by believing such nonsense."

Wu Hung told the Mandarin he believed in his charge, anyway. And left the courtroom in anger.

Hung determined to avenge his brother's death himself. He vowed to find Hsi Men and strangle him with his bare hands.

A man named Lee was a court secretary who was also an informer.

Lee knew he would receive a reward from Hsi Men if he got word to him fast about the happening in court and rushed as fast as he could to report that Wu Hung's case had been thrown out of court.

Hsi Men was, of course delighted with the news. He paid Lee five pieces of silver as a reward for the information and took him as his guest to his favorite wine house, The Golden Dragon.

The two men sat at a table on the exclusive second floor. They sipped wine, ate cakes, and were joined by a couple of painted song-girls.

Wu Hung's men had gathered information about Hsi Men for him and told him that the rich man's favorite wine house was The Golden Dragon.

Wu Hung, in his rage at the Mandarin's ruling, headed directly for the Golden Dragon in hopes he might be there.

Hsi Men was now particularly wary and on the alert. He kept glancing out the window as he was talking to Secretary Lee. And, with his constant vigilance, he caught sight of the husky captain raging down the street in the direction of the establishment.

Hsi Men knew immediately that his life was at stake and that he needed to escape. But he knew of only one way out of the establishment. And that was into the street where he would run right into the frightful Slayer of Tigers.

He was aware that there were a couple of office rooms up on the third floor of the building. In desperation, he decided that if he managed to get up there, he might evade the avenging giant.

Men told Lee, "Excuse me, Secretary. I have to leave you for just a moment. I'll be right back."

And with those words, he shot swiftly up the stairs.

At that moment, Wu Hung burst into the wine house and accosted the proprietor.

"Is Hsi Men here?" he stormed.

The proprietor knew better than to lie to the famed captain. "He's up on the second floor drinking wine with a friend," he revealed.

When Hung burst into the upstairs salon, the song-girls fled immediately and rushed downstairs. Informer Lee, however, remained glued to his chair in terror.

From his duty around the yamen, Wu Hung knew Lee was an officer of the court and that he had to be the one who had informed Master His about the ruling at the court proceedings.

He grabbed Lee by his jacket and pulled him upright.

"Where is that villain, Hsi Men?" he demanded.

Lee was shaking so hard he could not even find his tongue to speak.

Hung kicked over the table in his rage. Cups, plates, wine jars, wine and cakes spilled all over the floor with a loud crash.

Hung let loose of Lee's jacket waiting for an answer to his question. Lee tried to make for the steps leading downstairs and out the door to safety.

Hung grabbed the hapless secretary before he had even gotten out of arms reach. In his rage, he punched him in the face.

"Oh, no you don't get away that easy," he shouted. "Where is that villain Hsi?"

"I don't really know," Lee replied. "He just left."

Hung saw he wasn't going to get anywhere with the informer the way things were going. His wild rage increased. He lifted the terrified man off the floor by his pigtail, carried him to an open window and dangled him bodily out over the street below.

"Here's what you get, you miserable informer," he screamed at him. And with those words, he released Lee's pigtail and the informer fell to the street below.

Hung rushed about the premises looking for Hsi Men. He even looked upstairs.

But, by then, Men had looked out the window of the third floor office room where he was hiding. He saw a latticework of vines clinging to the outside wall. In desperation, he hauled himself outside the window and lowered himself, hand over fist, down into the courtyard of the next-door neighbor, a certain old Doctor Fu.

Hung looked out the window when he got upstairs, but by then the prey had disappeared into Doctor Fu's house.

When Hung failed to find his nemesis anywhere in the upstairs section of the wine house, he went storming downstairs. He still did not find him, so ran out onto the street.

There he saw a crowd around Secretary Lee. The informer was not dead, but was clearly dying.

In his anger, Wu Hung violently kicked the dying man. That action definitely killed the informant secretary.

One of the gawkers dared ask the giant, "Why did you kill that poor man?"

Hung snorted, "He was with Hsi Men. It was Hsi Men I intended to kill. My anger just got the better of me."

By then, the constabulary of the local ten-family association had arrived on the scene. The constables surrounded the rugged tiger-slayer and escorted him to the yamen.

News of the incident spread throughout the city. Soon there were false rumors. Including one that claimed that Hsi Men had been murdered.

When Hsi Men had escaped from the wine shop into the neighboring back yard, he crept surreptitiously along Old Doctor Fu's fence, trying to make himself as inconspicuous as possible. Just then, a maid came out of the house to head for the privy-hole. She was just squatting herself down when she spied the slinking aristocrat.

She screamed, "Thief, thief!" at the top of her voice, which brought the old physician out the door into his back yard.

Doctor Fu had stepped outside to see what all the hubbub was about, and was told about the apparent madman who was chasing after Master Hsi.

When he entered his backyard he recognized the nobleman by sight, of course.

"You are quite fortunate, Master Hsi," he exclaimed. "You have escaped capture by Captain Wu. He killed your companion and has been taken away to the district court. He will no doubt be convicted of murder and be beheaded. I'm sure you have no reason to try to stay hidden any more. You can walk right out onto the street and go home now."

Which is exactly what Hsi Men did.

As soon as he arrived back home, Men told Plum Blossom everything that had happened. The couple found the developments good cause to celebrate.

Men grabbed Plum Blossom by the waist and whirled her around. Her silk gown flew open, showing her lovely legs.

A gardener outside in the park was up a ladder pruning a tree. He heard Plum Blossom's joyful shriek and spied, through the window, a flash of golden thigh and a heady glimpse of a pubic triangle.

He was so overwhelmed by the sight that he leaned backward, upsetting the ladder. Both he and the ladder fell to the ground with a loud crash.

Plum Blossom heard the gardener's scream and the sound of the crash.

She looked out the window to try to see what was happening. "Shouldn't we close the drapes?" she asked her ready lover.

"No, my dove. We have nothing to hide," Men told her.

His proud manhood was standing at full attention and would not be thwarted by whatever was going on outside. As he lowered Plum Blossom to the floor, her clothing fell off. She, in turn, tore off his trousers as she went down. And, on her way, she managed to give a grazing kiss to his throbbing member.

Master Hsi picked his lover up and carried her to the bed and dropped her there. As she bounced, her legs flew wide apart. The moisture gracing her love opening gave witness to her readiness.

As Hsi Men sought entry, Plum Blossom giggled and playfully guarded her tunnel of love from entry. Men jovially growled at her.

Meanwhile, the gardener had carried his ladder back to the pavilion and was peeking in the window. And, my! What a sight he did behold.

He got so excited by what he was witnessing that he could not restrain himself from vigorously entertaining his own pride and joy with an uncontrollable fist.

Hsi Men responded to Pear Blossom's ploy and managed to push her guardian hand away from its feint and thrust his charger directly into the breach. His lover screamed in delight.

At that exact moment, the gardener's testicles convulsed, sending his pearl-colored stream splashing against the supporting wall.

Inside the room, the lady was clawing her husband's back as his hips pounded into hers. He playfully kissed and bit her neck with love nips.

As his love elixir spurted into her waiting womb, she spasmed like exploding fireworks while the gardener and his ladder toppled over onto the ground.

When the couple recovered, they looked out the window and saw the gardener running away as fast as he could with his pants at half-mast.

They grabbed onto each other in raucous laughter, ready to go at it again.

When the couple later sat down to discuss what had happened at the yamen, Plum Blossom wisely suggested that Hsi Men send fifty talents of silver and an elaborate silver wine service to the District Mandarin immediately, before he sentenced her captain ex-brother-in-law.

The next day, Wu Hung was brought before the Mandarin for his hearing. The Mandarin was clearly of a different mind from that expressed at the previous hearing.

"Captain," he said harshly. "Yesterday you bore false witness against worthy, respectable subjects of the Son of Heaven. I treated you then in a kindly fashion. In turn, I see that you have repaid my kindness by committing murder. And the victim was an esteemed officer of this court.

"What do you have to say for yourself?"

"I have a legitimate grievance against Hsi Men," Hung replied.

"It was unfortunate that Secretary Lee got in my way when I was in pursuit of my foe. My only petition to the court is that you have Hsi Men arrested so that the wrong committed by him might be righted."

"What you say, Captain, is senseless," the Mandarin replied. "The murder of Secretary Lee is quite independent of your grudge against Master Hsi. Do you confess to the murder?"

"No, your honor," Hung replied. "I will never confess to anything until Hsi Men's murder of my brother has been honestly dealt with."

"I see you are an obstinate fellow," the Mandarin scolded.

"We will see if a good beating won't make you confess."

Four of the court bailiffs grabbed Wu Hung and threw him to the floor. While two held him down, the others thrashed him fiercely with bamboo rods.

After twenty strokes, Hung was allowed to stand up and face the Mandarin.

Hung reminded the Mandarin of the worthy service he had performed for the court as captain of the guard.

That was not what the Mandarin wished to hear and he ordered not only fifty additional applications of the rods, but an application of the dreaded finger-press as well.

After the physical punishments were administered, a heavy wooden collar was affixed about Wu Hung's neck and he was thrust back into prison.

The current court secretary, one of the recipients of Hsi Men's largess, drew up a false confession and the Mandarin had four other court officers sign it.

The false confession stated that Wu Hung had demanded payment of 3,000 yuan from Secretary Lee for an old debt. And that he had strangled him in a murderous rage. Hsi Men's name did not appear at all in the alleged confession.

The following week, Prefect Chen made his quarterly visit to the District Court. His fairness as a juror was uncontested.

As he examined the cases that had been tried since his last visit, he questioned the trial of Wu Hung.

He called the accused and the witnesses to the confession to appear before him.

The prefect asked Wu Hung about the circumstances surrounding Secretary Lee's death.

"Honorable Master," Hung replied. "I have not hitherto been allowed to honestly state my case."

"You may now openly do so, Captain," the prefect told him.

Wu Hung proceeded to tell the story of his brother's murder, openly, naming Hsi Men and Plum Blossom as the miscreants.

He concluded by saying, "Since my petition for justice was thwarted in this court, I was obliged to avenge my brother's death myself. My vengeance was aimed at Hsi Men. By a regrettable accident, I killed Secretary Lee instead. If convicted of murder, I am prepared to accept the death penalty for the sake of my brother."

"I feel that I now understand this case perfectly," the prefect said when he had heard Hung's testimony.

He sentenced the court secretary who prepared the false confession to twenty strokes by bamboo rods. And he totally altered the confession document with his own brush.

The prefect announced to the court, "I find Wu Hung guilt of robbing Secretary Lee of his life and he must be punished. I also find that there are mitigating circumstances, so I rule that the current collar he is wearing is too harsh a punishment. Remove the heavy collar from Captain Wu's shoulders and replace it with the lighter one prescribed for those with lesser offences."

He referred the entire case back to the mandarin to be re-tried in open session, interrogating Hsi Men, Plum Blossom, Mother Wong, Brother Yuen and Coroner Hu Kiu.

Wu Hung remained in confinement awaiting the new trial. But he was very well treated by the jailors and was well supplied with wine and fine foods.

A court informer hastened to let Hsi Men know what had transpired at court.

Men knew the prefect was incorruptible. So he couldn't bribe his way out of the new situation.

So he decided to get Marshal Yang, a personal friend of his at the Eastern Capital, to intercede for him.

The marshal was not only a friend, but was deeply indebted to Master Hsi.

So, by means of bribes and favors, the court of the Son of Heaven passed a sentence decreeing that Captain Wu Hung was guilty of the murder of Secretary Lee. But the penalty for the crime was not to be death. Instead, the prisoner was to receive forty lashes, be branded and was to be banished to a military station at the Great Wall, two thousand miles away from the province where the crime took place.

The case was now closed.

The next day, forty lashes were administered to Wu Hung as directed from the Eastern Capital. The wooden collar was removed from his neck and shoulders and an iron one was riveted on in its place. Two rows of characters were branded on his cheeks. And, finally, closely guarded, he was marched off to the distant station at the Great Wall.

The news of all this was met with great joy by Hsi Men and deserved appropriate festivities in his park.

Near Plumtree House, His Men had constructed a party building, the Water Lily Pavilion. The disappearance of Wu Hung to the farthest reaches of the Celestial Empire deserved celebration at the new pavilion.

Musicians, dancing girls and song-girls were hired to entertain the crowd. A lavish banquet was prepared. The most exclusively prominent subjects and their wives were invited to attend the festivities.

At the head table, Hsi Men and his five wives were seated. His entire staff was seated behind the host and hostesses. The glamorous guests were seated around at teak and ivory tables. The rarest of wines were served in jade goblets. Rare dishes of dragon liver, phoenix giblets, bear paws and camel feet were served on crystal plates. The entertainers enhanced the rollicking mood.

It was the most lavish feast served in the province in recent memory.

Midway through the celebration a page entered the pavilion and introduced two attractive children, a boy and a girl attired in gorgeous silk garb.

The page announced, "Your neighbors, the Hua family, send flowers and cakes for the wives of Master Hsi."

The children kowtowed before Hsi Men and Moon Lady, then stood and stepped back.

The girl announced, "Our Mistress, Madame Hua Ping, sends flowers to serve as decorations for Master Hsi's wives' hair."

The boy then announced, "She also sends, as well, celestial cakes such as those served at the Imperial Court for the delectation of the ladies."

Moon Lady thanked the children and asked them to express her deepest thanks to their mistress.

"Madame Hua has shown courtesies to our house several times, recently," Moon Lady told Men. "I must return appropriate courtesies to her. But, somehow, I know very little about the lady. Can you tell me anything about her?"

"Master Hua married Mistress Ping about two years ago," Men told her. "The lady was Number One Concubine of the imperial secretary. So she brought a nice fortune to our neighbor when he married her. And a great deal of culture, as well. We must be sure to return the courtesies she has offered very soon."

Master Hsi had been good friends with Master Hua for some time, now. But the incident of Madame Hua's gifts to Moon Lady at the banquet ushered in a new era of neighborly involvement.

THE DEFLOWERING
OF ROSEBUD

The celebration of the banishment of the Tiger Slayer of King Yang Mountain continued until dark. And by the time the last guest left, Master Hsi was royally drunk.

He staggered from the festival pavilion to Plumtree House to top off the celebration with a bit of libidinous frolic. Plum Blossom knew to expect him and had the bed prepared and the incense burning.

The couple undressed each other and snuggled in under the perfumed silk sheets.

Plum Blossom was ready for love. But the excess of wine into which Men had engaged had robbed him of his masculine potency.

His worm hung flaccid. And, unfortunately, even Plum Blossom's expert oral and manual ministrations failed to arouse the dragon.

Hsi Men and his favorite wife sat up in bed, shed the sheets and Hsi called for a pot of tea.

Rosebud, the maid, entered the room clad only in her clinging silk nightgown. The sight of the maid's unused nipples outlined behind the translucent silk excited Men.

The couple was stark nude above the sheets and their legs were intertwined. Plum Blossom felt embarrassed by the sight exposed to her maid and started to draw the bedcurtains.

"Don't be silly, Dear," Men corrected her. "I know for a certainty that our next door neighbors, Hua and his wife Ping, disport themselves all the time in front of their young chambermaid. As a matter of fact, Hua even involves himself carnally with the maid at times. Quite a sport, that Hua."

"So that's what you have in mind, you rascal," Plum Blossom playfully scolded. "I am no more of a prude than Madame Ping. If you want to play your games with my virginal maid, be my guest. Not tonight, of course. Your dragon is asleep for the night. Tomorrow, though, I will be occupied elsewhere. Rosebud will still be serving here at Plumtree House. Deal with the situation as you wish."

Hsi Men kissed his wife and thanked her profusely. Rosebud blushed from head to toe, but was pleased beyond belief.

The order for tea was forgotten and the lovers fell asleep in each other's arms.

As we know, Rosebud was no stranger to the amorous cavorting of her master and her mistress. She had often lurked in the shadows and witnessed the festive rompings that went on in the bedchamber. For a long time, she had even longed to be able to play the fascinating games with her master herself.

When she lurked in the shadows watching, her delicate fingers always fluttered around the rim of her pleasure bowl. And, more often than not, she inserted an inquisitive finger in and out of the welcoming passageway she had come to feel very fond of. When she inserted her finger, she stopped short of rupturing the curtain within. That, she knew, should await the entry of a masculine tower like that possessed by the master.

The morning after the big party, before leaving the bedroom for the day, Plum Blossom advised Rosebud on how to pretend total innocence to the master in order to allow him to fully enjoy the seduction scene. As her mistress described in detail the impending course of action, thrills emanated from the maid's palpitating heart to her tingling crotch. She knew it would all be such fun actually doing *it*.

That evening, when Hsi Men arrived at the bedroom, he found the bed loaded with fragrant flowers. And, amidst the floral display lay the nubile nude body of the little maid. She shrugged and emerged from the lavish bouquet as her exquisite shoulders and perky young breasts came into full view.

Her soft tawny skin radiated youth. The soft, blue-black silky triangle that drew attention to the mound above her thighs dazzled the rake.

As Men stepped toward her, she coyly sank back down into her pool of flowers, allowing their coolness to recover her maiden body.

It had been a long while since Hsi Men had had the pleasure of deflowering a true virgin. The excitement that overcame him restored the feelings of anticipation he remembered from his youth.

He quietly removed his robe, and, naked, sat down on the edge of the bed. Rosebud observed his well-muscled body with newfound feelings. She was keenly aware of his aroma; his male muskiness was abetted by scents of aromatic oils.

Rosebud demurely pushed away the fragrant flower petals from her chest, revealing and offering up her lovely maidenly breasts for her master's delectation.

"O Master Hsi," she exclaimed, "I hope you love my breasts. I, myself, love them well. I fondle them tenderly when I am by myself. I pleasure them and in return they pleasure me. I long to kiss them but my lips cannot reach. They are too far away to get down there. They so long to be kissed."

Hsi Men accepted the invitation and bent his head over her left breast and kissed the tender nipple. As he did so, Rosebud wrapped a hand behind his head and ran her fingers lovingly through his hair. And she gently pressed his head down into the sucked teat.

Rosebud's tender, virgin nipple responded to Men's expert sucking and licking by pebbling up.

Men's right hand fondled the other breast, then slipped down to graze her abdomen. He followed by softly brushing her silken pubic bush.

As his hand slipped between the maiden's spread legs, her hand simultaneously gave up playing with his hair and landed softly, ever so gently, on the mast that had hoisted itself from his loins. She petted it as if it were a gentle kitten.

Men responded by raising his lips to hers and kissing them ever so tenderly. When she responded by kissing him back, he subtly inserted the tip of his tongue into her mouth.

Rosebud slipped her tongue under his and extended it into her seducer's mouth.

His hand slipped over her silken mound and traced a pattern around her moist, fragrant, virgin nether lips. She squirmed with pleasure at the soft massaging motion of his practiced fingers.

Master Hsi's two hands now kneaded and spread the outer lips of her vagina as a subtle finger lightly grazed her trembling clitoris.

The master positioned himself between his maid's spread legs, leaned down and nibbled at her sensuous neck. Spreading her labia apart, he positioned the pulsating head of his mast to where it could kiss her waiting love passageway. Then, grabbing her shoulders, Men signaled that the moment was at hand. And with a lunge of his hips, he drove through the guardian membrane into the depths of Rosebud's love garden.

Pain and pleasure converged as her eyes filled with tears of joy. His fleshly pillar churned agony into ecstasy.

Then, with a final thrust, Men's courser ejaculated its molten discharge into Rosebud's newly deflowered orgiastic cavity.

His sweat-drenched body fell to her side.

Tears streamed from their eyes while smiles lightened up their faces.

And the flowers that underlay their coupling were drenched in virgin blood.

From that moment on, Rosebud enjoyed an elevated position in the Hsi household. All menial tasks were removed from her duties. Making beds, serving tea and pleasing the master's whims now constituted the sum of her duties.

Plum Blossom gave Rosebud clothes and jewelry from her own belongings. And she taught her how to bind her feet.

Plum Blossom well knew that her reaction to Men's lust for the little virgin enhanced her own place in the master's estimation.

Pear Blossom was now, at last and without doubt, Hsi Men's favorite wife.

THE VIRGIN TOW GIRL

A week after the party celebrating Wu Hung's banishment to the Great Wall, Master Hua – Master Hsi's neighbor and long-time friend – threw a party for a group of his acquaintances. One of the guests he invited was Hsi Men. Men was particularly happy to go to the affair because he wanted to ask Hua to express his thanks for the courtesies his wife, Mistress Ping, had extended to Moon Lady.

Hua's party was held in a splendid pavilion in the park surrounding the Hua mansion. There were two gorgeous song-girls present as entertainment for the guests. The girls danced gracefully and played the pipa, the lute and the flute expertly.

The lithe girls were garbed in translucent white silk gowns. Their hair was upswept alluringly. Their tiny red mouths emitted the tips of their pink tongues at the conclusion of each number. And their powdered faces were graced by apricot colored cheeks.

There was not a guest present whose lust was not pleasantly stirred by the performance. When it concluded, the performers kowtowed to the admiring gentlemen. The audience members showed their appreciation by gifts of silver. Hsi Men, whose enjoyment of the girls' performance was enhanced by the liberal servings of fine wines his host had provided, raved with enthusiasm at the entertainers.

Hua laughed heartily at his friend's enthusiasm.

He chuckled and said, "The girls are a couple of tow girls from the Flower Garden District. You haven't been at the tow house with me in a long time, old friend. But I go there regularly to visit Silver Bird. She's the one who was playing the lute. She's my little darling. And last time you saw her, we were both deep in our cups.

"The other girl – Cinnamon Petal – happens to be the niece of your Number Two Wife, Sunflower. And I'll bet you didn't even know she had a niece down in the District."

Men regretted he had not remembered Cinnamon Petal. He and Hua used to go cavorting together in the Flower Garden District. Somehow, they hadn't done so for a while. Men decided he was going to make up for lost time.

When the last guest had left the pavilion, Hua and Hsi mounted their horses and escorted the girls back to the District. When they got to Cinnamon Petal's house, the two gentlemen were warmly greeted by her older sister who invited them in.

The girls' mother came in and set the table with food and drink. When she had everything set up for the men she discretely left and Cinnamon Petal made her entrance. She had changed clothes and was even more appealing than she had been before. While the gentlemen ate and drank, the girls sang, danced, played the pipa, the lute, the dragon flute and the rhinoceros drum.

Hsi Men said he would like to hear Cinnamon Petal do a solo. He waggled his eyebrows as he said so. Everyone knew what he really meant by a solo. And it had nothing to do with singing.

His request, and the way he made that request, was Cinnamon Petal's cue to bow graciously and leave the room.

Her sister explained to Men that Cinnamon Petal needed to go prepare her voice. Master Hsi placed several silver pieces on the table.

"I would like you to receive this little gift from me for cosmetics for your sister," he explained. "Later, when I know her better, I shall see that she can buy expensive silk gowns with gold embroidery."

"My sister's virgin flower is intact, dear Master," the sister told him. "You may, indeed, hear her sing and watch her dance. You may gift her with silk raiment. But you must know that only an extravagant gentleman can expect to receive back in return the gift that a maiden can only give once in her life."

Hsi Men understood perfectly. And his interest in the tow girl increased mightily. Cinnamon Petal was listening from behind a panel. She re-entered the room, bowed graciously and sat down.

"My sister has prepared her voice to perform her solo, if it please you, Master Hsi." The sister announced. Men indicated that it would, indeed, please him.

Cinnamon Petal was perfectly poised. She accompanied her lilting singing on the pipa. She laid down her instrument and danced beautifully, accompanied only by her voice. Her figure was as slim and supple as a willow branch. Her gestures were circumspect, and yet had hidden nuances. She covered her face with her hanging sleeves, yet peeked out with what could be interpreted as an invitation. She waved and fluttered her red silk scarf in a manner that caused obvious quivers to stir at Maser Hsi's groin.

Men grew so excited that he was even salivating. Her performance threw him into a state of rapture. Nothing would do other than having the lovely virgin at any price.

When Hua left the tow house to go find his paramour, Silver Bird, Men remained behind to spend the night with Cinnamon Petal's sister.

The overnight stay was more than just a toss in the hay for Hsi Men. In addition to the joys of the boudoir, he agreed to a price of fifty talents of silver for the gift the object of his affections could only give once. When he returned home the next morning, he told Number Two Wife, Sunflower, about his transaction of the previous evening.

Sunflower was delighted when she learned that her niece was to be honored by being deflowered by Master Hsi. She promptly sent a gift of fifty pieces of silver to her sister, Cinnamon Petal's mother, to help defray the expenses of food, wine, music and decorations for the celebration.

The delight that Hsi Men would derive from his coupling with Cinnamon Petal cannot be expressed. Deflowering Rosebud had been a tremendous delight. But Rosebud had not been trained from birth in how to delight a man in the rite of mutual seduction.

Cinnamon Petal was born a tow girl in a house of joy. She had been instructed in every artifice that makes blind fools of men. Every move she made was seductive. Her loins – perfumed by Nature herself – enveloped every would-be swain and drove him to madness. And few men were as avid voluptuaries as Men. He had spent his entire lifetime sharpening his appreciation for the sensuous attractions of the lovely sex. He was a connoisseur. And Cinnamon Petal was a choice, choice morsel.

The celebration of Cinnamon Petal's deflowering at the house of joy was grandiose. Hsi Men invited his most intimate friends. And Cinnamon Petal's mother and sister invited their most generous clients to attend as well.

The celebration began in the downstairs dining room, with Cinnamon Petal and Hsi Men at the head table. There was food and wine in abundance. Tow girls from neighboring houses entertained. Among them, of course, Hua's lovely item, Silver Bird.

At the appropriate hour, Cinnamon Petal and Hsi Men excused themselves and proceeded upstairs to raucous applause and shouts of the guests to the occasion. When they arrived at the boudoir, the room was well incensed. Flowers abounded all around. The couple smiled at each other as they approached the bed, which was covered with jasmine-scented silk sheets.

Hsi Men was delighted with the panoply of erotic ploys his little virgin possessed. Her small, dainty mouth was skilled in activities beyond mouth-kissing. Her joy-purse announced its readiness by its moist, murky redolence. She knew to expect a stealthy finger to enter her brown starfish at just the right moment. She even guided it there, to Men's delight. She did not lie stupidly with her legs extended in a V. Instead, her knees pressed up into her breasts, opening and exposing her silky saddle for her swain's easy attack.

Hsi Men was absolutely drunk with love when he broke through the virginal membrane and ejaculated his molten lava into the newly liberated channel.

The experience was worth everything Hsi Men had expended. He knew he had received his money's worth.

A FLING WITH PING

Hsi Men remained at the house of joy for several weeks. At length, though the deflowered tow girl's charms lost some of their novelty. As he grew bored with his newly acquired lifestyle his friend Hua's practice of visiting his Silver Bird as an occasional treat appealed to Men as a prudent practice. So he returned home to his five wives and to his business affairs.

A week after his return home, his friend Hua invited Men to come over to see him at home. Men knew pretty well that his dissolute friend had a little visit to the District planned and wanted his company.

Men arrived at the Hua residence at noon absorbed in thoughts about some business transactions he was involved in. Mistress Ping – Hua's wife – happened to be standing in the inner court when he arrived, and Men nearly ran right into her.

He had only seen Mistress Ping once before, when he had visited Hua's place. But on this occasion, because of the near-collision, he stepped back, bowed, excused himself, and ogled his friend's lovely wife.

In the heat of the day, she was scantily dressed in a light, white silk outfit. Her blouse was open at the throat and the outline of her bosom left little to Men's imagination. Her tiny slippered feet peeked out beneath her tight skirt. Men enjoyed what he saw of her full figure and admired her beautiful oval face.

Hsi Men, at that moment, was smitten by his neighbor's wife. He apologized to her for his clumsiness and was assured by her that no apologies were needed. That he was welcome to the Hua household as if it were his own.

She led him into the parlor and had a maid bring him tea. Mistress Ping sat down opposite him and joined him.

"My husband just stepped out for a moment to take care of a business emergency that took place," she told him. "He will be back shortly.

"While we wait for his return, may I make so bold as to ask a favor of you?"

"Whatever you wish, dear madam," Hsi Men responded gallantly.

"I believe my husband invited you over today because he wishes you to join him to visit a certain establishment in the Flower Garden District to partake in wine drinking.

"I would be very indebted to you if you would encourage him not to spend too long a time away there. You see, I am all alone in the house here with only my two maids, and quite vulnerable–" Madame Hua had not quite finished her sentence when Master Hua returned.

Men was preparing to answer her and tell her that he would do his best to comply with her request. But Hua's return cut him short. When Hua entered the parlor, Ping bowed herself out.

As he settled down opposite Men, Hua told his friend that his favorite tow girl, Silver Bird, was celebrating her birthday that very day. And he said he would like Men to accompany him to the party.

And, he whispered slyly, that Cinnamon Petal would very likely be present at the occasion.

The enticement of Cinnamon Petal was not too compelling to Men just then. But the prospect of bringing Hua back home to his wife early and thus making points with her was very appealing indeed. So Hsi Men told his friend he would be enchanted to join him for a bit of wine quaffing in the Flower Garden District and the two headed there without further delay.

When they got to Silver Bird's house of joy, it happened that Cinnamon Petal was not at the party. But that was of no consequence to Men. His aim was to get his friend stinking drunk as fast as he could and get him back home to his wife as soon as possible.

Silver Bird, as it happened, was as interested in getting her patron drunk as Men was. The drunker Hua was, the more generous he was. Before two hours were up, Hua was very drunk indeed. He had lavished three pieces of silver on his tow girl, and was soused enough that he did not protest when Men urged him away from the place and back to his home. There was no way, in his condition, that he could do any good in bed with Silver Bird anyway.

Mistress Ping was waiting at the door for her husband and his friend and favored Men with a word of thanks enhanced by a smile that held great promise.

From that beginning, Master Hsi had a scheme. And it worked beautifully.

He made it profitable for two of his less than upright acquaintances, who dwelled in the Garden District, to keep Hua entertained every time he visited a house of joy. The two men,

Wang Ying and Yat Ta, performed such vital services throughout the District as procurement of girls, providing opiates, or any other nefarious task that resulted in a positive cash flow to themselves.

Being paid generously by Master Hsi to keep Master Hua in his cups and away from home overnight was pleasantly remunerative for them.

Men and Hua became regular drinking buddies. They set out for houses of joy together at least two nights a week. Wang Ying and Yat Ta had no trouble finding out which house the friends patronized on any given night. They were on intimate terms with all the tow houses. After the drinking buddies appeared at any of the flesh peddling establishments, Men slipped away and the boys saw to it that Hua was being well entertained by a tow girl and was totally losing himself in drink.

When he got back to his neighborhood, Men loitered in front of his house and kept an eye out for Mistress Ping next door. The two merely exchanged meaningful glances the first few times. Hsi Men knew that once Ping was sure that her husband would not return until morning that she would make her move. But it took her a couple of days to feel sure that such was the case.

The third night of Ping's wait for her husband's return, she sent her maid to her neighbor's gate with a message as he was loitering outside his front gate.

Spring Violet, the maid, approached the master and announced, "My mistress asks whether you might wish to sit in the arbor of your park next to the fence separating your property from Master Hua's. She says that the jasmine flowers are particularly fragrant by the fence this evening."

Men informed the maid he was very fond of the perfume of night blooming jasmine. Spring Violet returned and reported that fact to her mistress.

Master Hsi left his vigil at his front gate and repaired to the parklands that surrounded his residence. He sat at a table that was located close to the fence that separated his property from his neighbor's.

Moonlight flooded the scene and the scent of jasmine was close to intoxicating. In a short time, he saw the round face of Mistress Ping's maid, Spring Violet, bob up over the top of the wall. Her head made a courteous bow and disappeared.

Men dragged his table and chair over to the wall. He climbed from the chair up onto the table. And from the tabletop he was able to hoist himself over the wall and onto a corresponding table on the other side. And thence, from a nearby chair he was able to step down into the parklands of his friend Hua's property.

The young round-faced maid beckoned for him to follow her to a pavilion close to the main house. The exquisite Mistress Ping, attired in a loose-fitting pajama outfit, bowed formally to him. He returned the bow.

"I believe it is unlikely my husband will return tonight," she told him.

"I can assure you he will not," Men told her. "I have arranged for him to be immersed in pleasures of his own. You have seen ample evidence, I am sure, that I have that situation under control."

"I am most thankful," Ping replied. "Won't you join me for a taste of wine?"

Men assured her that he would love to do so.

The maid poured tiger bone wine into a single goblet and disappeared from the scene. As Men began to raise his cup to his lips, Ping came around and sat on his lap. And they both drank from the same cup.

As they consumed the wine, Men deftly removed his companion's clothing from her full-bosomed body. His hands explored those bountiful mounds until the coral tips of her nipples were fully extended. She arose from his lap and assisted him in removing his clothing and the couple progressed in proud nudity into the adjoining bedroom.

Before settling down onto the fragrant silken sheets, the pair faced each other. Men lubricated his fingers with saliva before reaching behind his lover and placing a hand on each of her buttocks, pulling her up against his erect phallus.

She held her face up to his, and as he pressed his lips to hers and inserted his tongue into her waiting mouth, he ran a finger up and down across her brown starfish. As his tongue met hers, he inserted a moistened finger into her rear channel. It caused her to giggle while their tongues were intertwined and as she felt his member throb against her silken triangle.

Ping stepped back, breaking the contact. She dipped a hand into a bowl of scented oil and lovingly took his heated member into her hand and caressed the shaft up and down. Then, oiling the other hand, she took the love-sack that hung beneath his member and cradled the dual stones contained within the sack gently in her delicate hands.

Men gazed at her lovely form bathed in the glowing moonlight.

Her armpit hair and her silken bush exuded the scents of female musk enhanced by ambergris. He sniffed her armpits as she massaged the love-stones in his scrotum. Then, he lowered his lips to her breasts and gently stroked her clitoris with a skilled finger as his passion rose while her other hand grazed the knob that topped his risen tower.

At his deep sigh, she released his privates, opened the orange silk bed curtains and bade him kneel on the bed. When he was knelt and facing her, her lips descended and sucked the spongy ripe plum that topped the tower, sipping and slurping voraciously.

Men's whole body responded in a paroxysm and he hoisted her up onto the bed and in a mad plunge sunk his tool into her moist yearning jungle.

Ping ground her thighs in an agony of delight and slithered her tongue into her lover's foaming mouth. Their pressure mounted until their mouths separated to emit screams, and from Men's charging courser a molten splurge erupted into her spasming garden of delight.

The lovers then fell into a swoon, side by side, panting. They were both soaked in perspiration. Ping reached for a towel by the bedside and each wiped the other dry.

When they recovered, and the fabled phoenix arose again from its ashes, Mistress Ping – flat on her back – reached her feet up over her head touching the bed with her toes. The target for her lover's passion pole was calling for attack. And the pole fairly flew into the wrinkled brown receptacle that lead into her very innards. When he had discharged his load, Ping lowered her legs, allowed him to climb over her prostrate body, to where the sack that dangled from the root of his member could descend into her waiting mouth.

She swallowed the sack and, as she sucked, she ran her tongue around each of the eggs that nested within. Men masturbated as his lover pleasured his love-stones and he ejaculated his viscous seed all over her face. Ping insisted that he lick the albumen off her face slowly with his tongue. He delighted in doing so.

At the first cock's crow, Hsi Men arose, dressed, went to the fence, climbed back over into his own park. When he returned to Plumbtree Pavilion, Plum Blossom asked him where he had been all night.

"I accompanied my good friend Hua to Mother Ng's wine house," he told her.

Plum Blossom wasn't sure she believed him. She somehow had her doubts.

A couple of days later, Plum Blossom was sitting in the open-air sewing with Jade Fountain in the afternoon. She happened to glance up at the property fence when she noticed a girl's head peeking over. The head popped back down immediately.

The furtive apparition aroused a tiny suspicion in Plum Blossom's mind. What was Mistress Ping's maid up to? Could it be possible...?

With her suspicions aroused, Plum Blossom decided to spy on her husband.

So, that evening, when he claimed to be going to visit his Number Three Wife, Jade Fountain. Plum Blossom slipped out into the moonlit night and furtively followed him.

Her husband's footsteps were not directed toward Jade Fountain's pavilion. Instead, they led towards the fence that bordered Neighbor Hua's property.

The moonlight reflected the same face she had previously seen pop up from behind the fence.

The next thing she saw was Men moving a table and a chair over to the wall. He climbed up then hoisted himself over the fence.

The next morning, Men dropped by Plum Blossom's bedroom to join her for morning tea. As soon as he entered, she dropped the bomb on him.

"Look, Men," Plum Blossom scolded. "I'm on to your little game with Mistress Ping next door. With my own eyes, I saw you hurling yourself over the fence. No lies now. Confess!"

Hsi Men knew he'd been caught. There was no sense denying it. Having sex with other women was no problem at all. It was perfectly legal and expected of him.

But an affair with a wife of a fellow aristocrat, a civic leader and a close friend. Knowledge of that would cause a scandal. He would lose face in the community. Indeed, throughout the province and beyond.

"Please, my dove," Men nearly whined. "No scandal. A scandal would do irreparable harm not only to me, but to you as well." Plum Blossom saw that she had her husband at a great advantage to herself.

"All right, Men," she said. "I will not disclose your disgraceful behavior. But, in exchange, you must promise me a few things."

"Whatever, light of my life. Just ask," he promised.

"First," she told him, "you must give up visiting the houses of joy. I do not like you going to enjoy tow girls. It is degrading to me." Hsi Men agreed, reluctantly. He was nearly addicted to the girls of the Flower Garden District. But to avoid scandal...

"Second," she demanded, "you have to obey me implicitly from now on. You are to treat me as if I were your Number One Wife." Hsi felt he could comply with that request in exchange for avoiding scandal. He agreed with her second condition.

"And thirdly," she declared, "after you return home from your little trysts with Madame Hua, you must tell me in detail every little thing the two of you do together. I will hear from you every ploy she engages you with, with her hands, her mouth, her breasts, her two lower orifices. Everything. And what's more, I want to hear exactly how those actions of hers affect you."

Actually, that last concept was rather pleasing to Men. To relive his experiences with Ping while recounting them to Number Five Wife would actually be pleasurable. Particularly when he knew that she would get turned on from hearing the positions the knowledgeable Ping had in her arsenal and she would be anxious to try them out with him.

So accordingly, for several months, Hsi Men avoided his tow girls. He bought Plum Blossom whatever presents she demanded. And he faithfully explained every detail that occurred between himself and Ping. And he gained the reward of demonstrating the positions Ping employed with his sexy wife.

A GLEESOME THREESOME

As the months wore on, Men began to weary of Plum Blossom's hold over him. He missed his tow girls, especially Cinnamon Petal. He hated being told by Plum Blossom what presents he should get her and when. And as for reporting his frolics in bed with Ping, eventually Plum Blossom did not take to them, and they were no longer amusing.

But one fine day – after a few months had passed by – Hsi Men received good news. It was reported to him that his neighbor, Hua, was in very ill health. Master Hsi sent Young Tai, his boy-servant, next door to inquire of the neighbor's health.

"Alas, Master," the lad reported back. "Mistress Ping's maid, Spring Violet, informs me that her master is at death's door. She says it is unlikely he will live another week."

What good fortune, Hsi Men thought. *If the bastard dies, there will be no possible scandal about my relationship with Ping.*

And I can have her all to myself without Plum Blossom being able to exploit the situation.

Little Tai was sent each morning to the property next door to inquire into Hua's health. The good news came within three days. Hua was dead. He was twenty-four years old.

Hello tow girls. Goodbye the ax Plum Blossom held over his head.

Young Tai continued to be sent to the Hua home every morning for news. And, of course, news of the prominent aristocrat, Hua, was on everyone's lips as well.

And the news got even worse – better for Men, though. Official proceedings following Hua's death proved that he had died bankrupt.

Hsi Men discussed Madame Hua's sad situation with Number One Wife. She suggested that he perform an act of charity in accordance with Buddhist teachings and purchase a modest house that the lady could live in. And, in addition, that he provide the widow with subsistence money.

Men thought that was a splendid idea. It would put Ping totally at his disposal. He relished that.

Before long, Ping sent Spring Violet to Men requesting him to come see her to give her advice on what to do in her new dire circumstances

When he arrived at her home, he could see that Ping was devastated. Not only was she left a widow, but a destitute one. All of Hua's property was forfeit to a host of creditors. She had no previous idea that her husband was seriously in debt. Neither did Hsi Men.

Ping asked her good neighbor (and sometime lover) what course she should now take. Of course, he and Moon Lady had discussed the matter so he had an answer at hand.

Men assured her he would see that she at least had somewhere to live. And that he would supply her with enough money to at least get along.

The very next day, Master Hsi did purchase a very modest house on Lion Street and gave the keys to Mistress Ping. She was very grateful and promised she would find a way to pay him back.

Men was confident she would. *Ha, ha.*

Once the widow and her maid were moved in, Men went to the house on Lion Street to visit the Widow Ping.

He sent ahead fine food and wine for the occasion. The house had been made fragrant with incense and an abundance of aromatic flowers.

The grateful widow thanked him again for his support.

"When my period of mourning is over," she asked him, "might you have a place in your household for a Number Six Wife? That way, this house could be sold and you would have your money back. And, I assure you, I would be a very loving and obedient wife."

Men was too wary to commit himself to the suggestion. He had plenty of time to think about it. It might or might not be the best way to get everything to his best advantage. So he said it was not appropriate to even consider such matters until the half year of obsequies, mourning and rites required by Buddhist tradition and legal dictates were complied with.

That answer kept him off the hook long enough to decide if that would really suit him.

"But in the meantime," he assured her, "I will send enough pieces of silver here to you to keep you well enough supplied to live quite comfortably." While they were talking, Spring Violet was preparing the delicious food.

After serving them to satiety, the couple retired to the bedroom. Ping believed a threesome might amuse Men enough to make him more enthusiastic about marriage. So she bid the maid accompany them into the boudoir.

"Spring Violet," she said sweetly. "Please assist Master Hsi in removing his garb." The request surprised Men. But gave him a thrill.

As Ping disrobed, Spring Violet removed the master's clothes in such a way that her lovely, supple hands and fingers played love dances all over his body. By the time he was nude, Men was aquiver with passion and was displaying a hotly pulsating erection.

"I must repay my lovely disrobing assistant by providing the same service to her," he said.

And with skill equal to that of the maid, he removed every stitch of her clothing. As he uncovered her nether-garment it revealed her blue-black love-nest.

Men slipped to his knees and buried his nose into it to inhale its fragrance. There is no scent more welcome to a randy connoisseur's senses than that of a young maiden's snatch. Mistress and maid each took a hand, raised the priapic master up onto his feet and led him to the purple curtained bed.

He lay on his back on the perfumed silk sheets, spread eagle, with his pride and joy reaching aloft at its fullest bloom.

Spring Violet stretched out with her head between his spread legs while Ping positioned herself with her mouth at her maid's joy-purse.

Spring Violet scooted up and enclosed Hsi Men's towering rod within her lips while her mistress flickered her educated tongue into her maid's fragrant humid garden of delights. While the maid sucked, she enclosed her lips tightly around the spongy tower-head and her girlish tongue played fairy-dances all around its surface.

All three bodies were approaching convulsions of joy. The three persons became one writing animal on the point of achieving rapture. Mistress Ping, who was the bottom half of the passion inflated monster, could tell from the increased flow of the dampness at her maid's crotch that the top portion of the triad, Master Hsi's palpitating charger, was about to discharge its life-giving elixir into the mouth of the mid-section of the three-part organism they formed. With a switch of position, Ping repositioned herself so her tongue would dart into Spring Violet's wrinkled brown orifice at the exact moment of the triple orgasm.

The inevitable reduction of Men's phoenix to the state of a limpid worm following his discharge rendered him useless just as the two women's passions sought further fulfillment. So while Hsi Men lay on his side, soaked with perspiration and panting, his bed companions – ignoring the useless state of his equipment – threw their heads into each other's crotches. Their supple tongues played frantic tattoos on their targets.

Men watched the action with excited eyes as the two women became a two-backed beast that writhed, rolled about, kicked and bounced all over the bed.

Spring Violet let out a piercing scream, convulsed in a giant orgasm, and dropped onto the bed surface in exhaustion. Mistress Ping, however, was still raring to go. The erotic spectacle Men had been observing caused a blooming resurgence at his crotch. He brought the member to high tension by stroking it with his agile fist.

Ping assumed the position of a bitch in heat, facing away from the newly aroused canine. With unerring precision, the dog-man aimed his ready puzzle into the awaiting anus and pounded into the passageway with an intensity and rhythm that shook the bed's surface, reviving Spring Violet. Ping – with a cry of exultation – collapsed onto the bed's surface as Men's manhood spurted its pearl-colored fountain onto the sheets.

Spring Violet was aroused by the sight of the moribund member and thrust herself into action for a final feast. She took the dying member into her mouth, emptying the fountain of its last remaining tasty droplets.

Hsi Men felt that his new relationship with Hua's widow was extremely fortuitous.

DOCTOR HU GETS
THE TREATMENT

Hsi Men left the house on Lion Street assuring the two women he would continue to provide for their financial needs and that he would return soon.

He was true to the first promise. He directed his banker to deliver a certain amount of silver every month to Madame Ping.

But as to the second promise, he was less than faithful.

He was not sure in his mind whether he really wanted a Number Six Wife or not. So – although he thoroughly enjoyed the threesomes he engaged in with Mistress Ping and her lovely maid – like with everything else, his interest began to wane. And, after a few months, he gave up visiting the house on Lion Street at all. And his absence from the house became a great concern to Madame Ping and her maid.

Ping sent Spring Violet to Hsi's home repeatedly. But no one even let her through the gate. Mistress Ping's health began to deteriorate.

The days of waiting to hear from Hsi Men weighed heavily on her. The days stretched into weeks. And the weeks lengthened out to months. True, Men's banker sent subsistence money to her every month. But the amounts dwindled bit by bit.

When the fifth month of Widow Hua's mourning arrived, the substance money simultaneously came to an end. She had suffered increasing nervous tension from the third month of waiting on. But – with the advent of the fifth month – her health was visibly faltering.

Her mistress's deteriorating health concerned Spring Violet a great deal. This turn for the worse alarmed her. So, on her own initiative, the maid contacted a doctor to come examine her mistress.

The physician, Dr. Hu Hee, was not a particularly appealing little man. He was thirty years old, had shifty eyes, and was a dissatisfied, horny bachelor. When he arrived, he shuffled over to the patient's bed, took her pulse and checked the state of her tongue. He shook his head and said, "Hmm…"

He had Spring Violet assist him in disrobing the pale, wasted-away body for further examination.

While there were signs of apparent weight loss, the lovely breasts were still quite prepossessing. He palpated each one with enthusiasm. He pinched the nipples. If Spring Violet were not still in the room, he would have medically examined their tension with his lips.

He ordered the maid to go boil some water for him. As soon as she was gone, he assured his patient that it was medically necessary for him to apply suction to the nipples.

Widow Hua did not object in the least.

Dr. Hu spread her legs apart to check her temperature at the humid, hair-fringed entrance that is known medically to be the most efficacious spot for such digital examination. With the educated fingers of each hand he felt the temperature both on the nether lips and up inside the moist tunnel.

Again, Widow Hua objected to the examination not in the least. The attending doctor judiciously grunted, tsk-tsked, hemmed, hummed and clicked his tongue.

Dr. Hu Hee was a very thorough examiner. When Spring Violet returned to the bedroom with the pot of hot water, the doctor gave his diagnosis.

"Widow Hua," he announced. "I regret to inform you that the Yin in your dantian is at variance with the Yang. The result has induced a bifurcation of the emanation from your spleen which had caused consternation in your womb. The result is a melancholy state which can only be cured by sensual applications. I have some herbs with me which should be steeped in the hot water your maid has brought up. And the pills, which also are in my satchel, should be taken thrice a day.

"I will return in three days to check up on you," he finished. The herbs and the pills were known for their aphrodisiacal qualities. The good doctor never made house calls without them.

After Dr. Hu had departed, Spring Violet brewed the herbs. Mistress Ping gulped down a goblet full of the brew, washing down a pill in the process.

Within a half-hour, Ping was already feeling much better. Her womb was gurgling happy sounds; her nipples perked up delightfully, and her crotch began to blaze with yearnings.

Spring Violet – at her mistress's command – applied oral pressure to the perked nipples, performed digital palpitation to the fully moisturized entry-to-heaven, and ended up giving lingual succor to the yearning crevasse. Then Ping's own needful lips and tongue enjoyed relief at her maid's bosom and crotch.

When Dr. Hu Hee returned on his follow-up visit, he found his patient totally recovered from her delicate condition and waiting for him in the front room.

With her renewed health and absence of melancholy, she came to the decision that it was foolish to count on Hsi Men for any kind of support. The doctor's ministrations had done her some good. Perhaps she should settle for matrimony with the ugly, horny, old bachelor.

"You are looking much better since I saw you last," he told her.

"Your herbs and pills gave me a very new lease on life, Doctor," Ping said. "I feel so much better now. All over."

As she said "all over," she brushed her hands suggestively over her breasts and pubis. The attentive doctor tented feebly beneath his cotton trousers.

Doctor and patient were, each, very attentive to the other.

"What would you prescribe for me to take in order not to fall back into the parlous condition you found me in last time you were here, Doctor?" Ping asked.

Dr. Hu decided on a brave new course.

"A lovely, charming lady like you would fare, physically – best – Madame... by considering matrimony," he answered.

Dr. Hu Hee was not a bachelor by choice. He had wanted a wife from the time he was twenty years old. But he realized that he was such a disgusting specimen of masculinity that he never dared propose. And he would never succumb to the indignity of buying a wife. So he got all his loving in the Flower Garden District. But he realized at that moment that the lovely Mistress Ping might actually be coming on to him.

His erection pulsed a bit. To have access to such a woman as this as wife and bedmate would realize his wildest dream. She would be not a purchased bride but a woman who came to him from love.

"Alas," Ping said. "I am but a poor desolate widow. I doubt that any man would consider taking me as wife." She sighed, disguising the disgust she felt for the hideous fool who appeared to be the last resort to get her out of what looked like a long, dismal state of penury.

The doctor responded, "I know of a man who, I am positive, would be enraptured were you to accept his proposal of marriage."

"If you know of such a gentleman," Ping said coyly, "I would deem it a favor were you to have him contact a matchmaker to come to me and present the traditional engagement presents and plead his client's case to me."

Dr. Hu fell to his knees.

"The man I am talking about has no need for a matchmaker. I myself am the man."

He prostrated himself on the floor and kissed her feet.

"I offer myself as a suppliant to ask you to be my wife," he said. "As an engagement present, I offer you three talents of silver to purchase whatever your heart desires." He burst into tears, blubbering revoltingly. Mistress Ping looked down on the wretch convulsing at her feet.

What a disgusting piece of offal he was. But three talents of silver? The security of being the wife of a prosperous doctor. Was the price worth sharing the marriage bed with such a despicable creature worth it?

The answer was a reluctant yes. She thought she had better seal the offer with a romp in the adjacent bedroom. She reached down and lifted the sobbing, giggling sap to his feet.

"Come," she said. "I gratefully accept your offer. Let us celebrate our engagement with a pre-nuptial conjugal union." Ping led the way to the boudoir, swishing her hips seductively. Hu wobbled along behind her, drooling and all agog.

Once in the bedroom, as Ping removed her jewelry and undressed, Hu sat on the floor ogling, attempting to get his own clothes off.

With the tow girls whose favors he had bought, he was not helpless. He paid well and felt he deserved what he got. The girl always helped him out of his clothes and serviced his somewhat unreliable member with slurps and finger play. In the presence of the priceless Widow Hua, however, he was a helpless mess.

She helped him to his feet and assisted him to get his clothes off. He was shaking like the leaves of the li tree.

He was overcome by the splendor of her pink tipped breasts, her slim waist and her silky pubis. He had probed her body when she was his patient and his member had grown somewhat turgid on that occasion. Now, as her would-be lover – her husband-to-be – the flaccid worm that drooped from his groin was totally unresponsive

Ping was well versed in the arts of love, and with spittle and wanking, she managed to get the feeble worm worked up into a semi-hardness sufficient to penetrate her cold flue. It was a total relief for her when he managed to spurt his feeble contents into her dry love-purse.

As poor a performance as it was, the doctor was profusely thankful. The newly engaged couple proceeded from the bedroom to the Buddhist sanctuary and from there to the yamen to solemnize their union. Dr. Hu Hee moved himself and his belongings into the house on Lion Street that very afternoon.

A week later, with gentle coaxing and coaching by his wife, the good doctor's performance eased up to where he was as adept with his manhood as he had been with the tow girls he had previously hired. At least that was a relief to his now pecuniary solvent wife.

And within a week, he opened a new, modern dispensary and clinic in what had previously been the front room of the house. With the splendid new office and dispensary, business improved.

When Hsi Men heard that Mistress Ping had married Doctor Hu, the news enraged him.

True, he had pretty well rejected and abandoned Ping. But the thought of her marrying a rival herb dispenser – and a repugnant one at that – annoyed him deeply. He had to get revenge. Revenge on whom? On that quack of a doctor, of course. So he went to the Flower Garden District and made contact with those notorious hirelings, Wang Ying and Yat Ta.

He invited them to join him in a cup at a nearby wine house. They were pleased to accept the gentleman's invitation. When the attendant had disappeared from earshot, Master Hsi reached into his purse and dropped ten pieces of silver onto the table.

"Do you know where that wretched Dr. Hu Hee has opened his new office and dispensary on Lion Street?" he asked.

The two ruffians nodded assent.

"The quack has insulted me greatly," Men continued. "I would be pleased if he were taught a good lesson in manners. Anonymously, of course. I would not care for him to know that I am behind the lesson in any way." Wang Ying scooped up the silver and slipped it into his satchel.

"We would be quite pleased to serve as teachers to the blackguard doctor," he told the master.

"Those paltry pieces of silver are just tokens of my friendship for you two notable righters of wrongs," he said.

"If the lesson is delivered effectively, there will be triple that amount."

"Be assured, Master Hsi," said Yat Ta, "within the time of three sunsets, you shall be avenged for the wrong the filthy rat has done you." The three men polished off their cups and departed the shop.

When he arrived home, Men went to meet Plum Blossom in her pavilion. The deal he had closed with the two avengers had left him in good spirits and in a mood for love. The taste of wine was still in his mouth and he sent Rosebud to fetch a flagon of tiger bone wine.

When the maid returned and served the wine, her mistress was seated on the master's lap with his love pole inserted snugly in her fragrant garden. The maid served them their cups, which they downed while the mistress rode that pole as the couple laughed giggled and gasped. Rosebud was invited to remain, serve and watch the proceedings while fingering her vulva. She did not leave the scene until the master and the mistress shook with orgasms. Half drunk, the couple made its way over to the bed and romped and tossed until dawn.

Madame Hu's attempts to teach the horny but inept Dr. Hu the amorous arts met with limited results. In part, the problem was of her own making. She could not stand the man. She introduced Spring Violet to the doctor's bed. The maid was able to get an adequate rise from Hee's flagpole.

But Ping did not feel that was an adequate solution to her husband's insufficiencies. So she sent the maid to the Flower Garden District to summon two tow girls to the house. Dr. Hu had a noisy orgy with them. But because of the repugnance she had for her worm of a husband she could not bear to so much as look at him anymore. And as far as kissing or fondling him or allowing him any form of intimacy was concerned, it was out of the question.

Ping still longed for Hsi Men and wondered how she had lost him. What had she done? She longed for the glorious lovemaking of her life before she married her flop of a husband.

Dr. Hu took refuge from his wife's sour moods by retreating to his herb and pill dispensary in the former front room of the house.

One morning when Dr. Hu Hee had retreated from his shrew of a wife into the safe haven of his clinic and dispensary, two rough-looking characters came bounding in and plunked their butts on the bench at the counter.

"What may I do for you two gentlemen?" the good doctor inquired.

Wang Ying replied jovially, "My friend here has a bad case of blue balls, Doc. He'd like some wank herb to cure it."

Dr. Hu looked perplexed.

"I'm afraid I am not acquainted with that particular herb," he said. "But, if I understand your friend's condition correctly, I have a supply of qian lie wan in stock. It is very efficacious."

Yat Ta broke in before the doctor had quite finished his sentence.

"Look, Doc," he said, "my homie here doesn't like to mention it. But he has a bad case of droopy dick. Just get us some hard-on pills and we'll be on our way."

Dr. Hu thought he had just the thing for that second slimy looking customer.

"Oh, yes," he smiled. "I'll get you some kang wei ling right away. It will straighten things out, so to speak, nearly immediately."

"Look, you old quack," Yat Ta growled. "Let's cut the crap. We were just fucking with your head. You know what we're really here for."

Hee was suddenly alarmed. He sensed danger. He attempted to answer in a normal voice despite the trembles that began to shake his body.

"I assure you that kang wei ling really will–"

"Fuck your kang wei ling," Ta yelled at him. "You know perfectly well that my pal is here to collect the thirty pieces of silver you owe him. Me and him hate deadbeats. You've held out on him for two years now. Well, the time's come and he wants back the money he lent you with interest. Get it?"

"You gentlemen obviously have mistaken my identity for someone else," the doctor stuttered. "I have never seen this gentleman in my life. I don't know who he is at all."

"You must have a real poor memory," Ta snarled. "You used to have that crappy little herb and pill store over on Tiger Lily Street. Back then you whined to my pal here that you needed thirty pieces of silver to pay for your grandma's funeral. Come on. It's payback time."

Wang Ying suddenly spoke up.

"Come on, Doc. You know me well enough. My name is Lu. I lent you thirty pieces of silver two years ago. With interest, that has mounted up to forty-eight pieces by now. I'm here to collect. Now!"

"This is preposterous," the little doctor said. "Show me the note." Yat Ta pulled a sheet of paper out of his sleeve and shook it in Hee's face.

"That's just a piece of–" Hee began.

For a response, Ta punched Hee right on the nose, smacking it to a pulp. Then he knocked over the showcase, breaking the bottles of herbs and pills. The floor was covered with leaves, stalks and pills.

A second blow sent the little doctor tumbling atop the mess. Yat gave him a good kick to the groin when he was sprawled out on the floor.

"There," he said. "Maybe that will help you remember to pay your debts next time." Dr. Hu's cry and the sound of the crash brought police into the shop. They led the three men off to the Yamen. Madame Hu observed the whole show from the upstairs landing with secret satisfaction. She hid her smile behind her fan.

As soon as Hsi Men got wind of what had happened, he sent word to his good friend, the provincial judge, who would preside over the case the next morning.

With the note, Men sent an appropriate sum of money.

The next morning when Dr. Hu was hauled into the courtroom, the judge asked him why he refused to pay his debt. And why he insisted on slandering the man who had so kindly lent him the money. The judge read a paper that he held up for all to see.

"This is a clear legal promissory note proving you borrowed the money. Your refusal to pay back your debt is reprehensible." He ordered that the doctor receive thirty strokes on his back, which were delivered forthwith.

The bailiffs then dragged the doctor to the house on Lion Street to collect the thirty pieces of silver. As an act of mercy, the interest was forgiven.

Wang Ying and Yat Ta, who had been freed by the judge telling them how sorry he was they had been incarcerated, accompanied the bailiffs and the prisoner.

If the silver was not forthcoming, the prisoner was to be led off to debtor's prison. Madame Ping met the contingent at the door of the house. Dr. Hu pled with her.

"Give these two gentlemen thirty pieces of silver so I can be freed."

She spit in his face and he was carried off to jail sobbing like a baby.

The whole affair had re-ignited Hsi Men's passion for Madame Ping. He went to her house and proposed to her. Her husband's incarceration freed her of her marriage to the despicable doctor.

Ping happily accepted the offer to be Number Six Wife.

A visit to the sanctuary and the yamen sealed the deal. And Hsi Men was – again – a bridegroom.

ECSTATIC PAIN

The re-surfacing of passion that Hsi Men felt for Mistress Ping was somewhat different from its previous manifestation. Previously, raw lust was the dominant issue. This time, the lust was powerfully tinged with sadism. For reasons he probably could not explain to himself, Master Hsi now planned to derive pleasure from Ping's suffering.

On the day following their marriage, Men sent a marriage litter with prominent silk draperies to the house on Lion Street to transport the bride to her new lodgings. She was carried through the streets in the litter proceeded by men carrying the traditional large orange lanterns.

When she got to the gate to the Hsi properties, the litter bearers and lantern wielders walked away, leaving her all alone in her contraption. Master Hsi sat upstairs inside the main house in casual clothes and looked down on his new bride. He had forbidden Moon Lady (who – as Number One Wife – had to be the official welcomer) to approach the bride until he specifically ordered her to.

Mistress Ping did not know what to do. No one came out from the building to meet or greet her. The sun beating down on the conveyance was uncomfortable. And Hsi Men was enjoying himself immensely at what he knew to be her embarrassment and discomfort.

He intended to enjoy his new wife in a hilariously new manner. Truth to tell, Moon Lady did not welcome this addition to the ménage, and secretly enjoyed the game her husband was playing with the hussy.

After three full hours of waiting, Master Hsi gave Moon Lady orders to go out and escort the new wife into the main building. Once Ping was out of the litter, servants were sent to haul it away. Hsi Men did not go downstairs to greet his new wife. He had told Moon Lady to conduct the newbie to a pavilion prepared for her in the park.

And all the rest of the day and all night, Number Six Wife was left alone in her new home. No one came to see her except a serving maid who bought her two modest meals.

Meanwhile, Hsi Men was having a riotous time with Plum Blossom in Plumtree House.

One day led to another. Despair overcame the bride… She was lonely, mortified, moaning, sobbing and forlorn.

On the third day of her cruel confinement when the maid came to deliver the morning meal, she found Mistress Ping – clad in her wedding raiment – hanging from the ceiling by her silk sash. The frightened girl rushed out the door to Plum Blossom's pavilion and relayed the news. Plum Blossom, accompanied by Rosebud, came to the rescue with a pair of scissors.

Plum Blossom cut the sash and she and Rosebud caught the body before it fell to the floor. Ping was still breathing. The silk noose she had fashioned was clumsily knotted and was incapable of strangling her.

When news was bought to Master Hsi, he gathered a rope and a whip and proceeded to Ping's pavilion.

When he entered her pavilion, Men found his bride sitting on her bed, her hands over her face, and blubbering softy. He accosted her angrily.

"So, Little Bride," he said with a sneer, "you decided to hang yourself. Fine! But it was extremely rude of you to choose to do so here at *my* place. If you were going to do yourself in, you could have shown the decency to do it back at the house on Lion Street. Which, you may recall, I was kind enough to provide for you when you were in sore need.

"But, my dear, if you really wish to hang yourself, do not let me hinder you. Look. I've even brought some good sturdy rope for you to do it with. It will make a good, effective noose that will do the job better than that silly silk sash you bungled the job up with before."

With that, he whipped her across the face with the rope, startling her. Ping gasped and choked off her sobbing. Rather than grief, actual fear reflected from her features.

"Now!" Men shouted. "Get on with it. Off that bed and off with those clothes."

Ping was frozen in space. She was confused and terrified. Men grabbed her roughly by the shoulders and dragged her off the bed.

"Off with your clothing, I said." Ping was clumsily able to remove her clothing with trembling hands. "Now, down on our knees! Now, I say!"

As she knelt down, Hsi Men took his horsehide whip in hand and, with marked precision, administered three lashes to her delicately rounded buttocks. As he did so, he experienced a surge of erotic satisfaction. His heart began to beat faster and the tingling sensation that originated in his crotch galvanized his entire being.

This feeling had been lurking within Master Hsi's soul from the moment his interest in Ping was re-kindled. He realized that it was this feeling of elation he had secretly hoped for when he decided to honor her as Number Six Wife.

A joyful rage overcame the bridegroom. He walked around her exposed naked body, flicking the cruel whip in a blind frenzy. Nothing was spared. The slashes at her nipples aroused an ecstasy in him. The blows that cut into her pubes were close to orgasmic for him.

Surprisingly, the orgasmic sensations were not one-sided. The pain Ping suffered was close to unbearable at first. It seared her to the very marrow of her bones. It was the strongest sensation she had ever suffered.

But, as one cruel stroke followed another, the pain morphed into a rare, new sensation. She knew pain and she knew pleasure. She knew titillation and she knew joy. But – for the first time in her life – she now felt ecstasy.

As her master beat her, the tears streaming down her face were transformed into rivers of exultation. When Men finally dropped his flail, Ping crawled over to him on her knees, pulled down his pants, removed his undergarment and faced his priapic member.

To her, it was a manifestation of the godhead. The master's staff was the lingam of the Indian God Shiva. It was to be worshipped.

She took the ripe plum that turbaned the lingam into her devoted mouth and laved it with tongue and lips. When it spent its holy seed into her mouth, she rose, kissed her lord and shared the elixir with her lover-god.

Convulsions of love washed over the newly conceived lovers.

Men lifted his lover in his arms and carried her to the bed. His mighty phoenix arose again and plunged itself into her dripping, moist love-purse.

Hsi Men did not leave the pavilion all day long. He remained enclosed therein all night as well. The couple engaged in one frenzied engagement after another, with the application of the whip keeping their ecstasy alive without surcease. The bedsheets were hopelessly covered and stained with streaks and pools of blood. A testimony to the divine love-feasts Men and Ping engaged in.

Mistress Ping enjoyed the master's favors thenceforth as the undisputed favorite. The pleasure/pain kept the couple in a jubilant state. Neither one could imagine a higher level of pleasure.

Then, one morning, Men and Ping picnicked in one of the arbors in the park. The cook had prepared special delicacies for the occasion and the steward had chilled a very nice wine to accompany the outdoor feast.

The cook sent the food and wine out to the arbor with Pink Aster, the young maid Hsi Men had given to his new favorite wife. The couple found the wine particularly pleasing and tended to consume enough to get tipsy.

Before leaving for the picnic, Men had the kinky notion to take along some stands of rope. His idea was only half-formed. But the wicked glint in his eye revealed to Ping that there just might be mischief afoot.

The arbor they went to was in a secluded spot and Ping, anticipating a possible quirk in store, was feeling wanton enough to shed her clothes. Hsi Men watched her undress with enjoyment. The provocative way in which she had done so had the effect of causing his member to stand up and salute.

"I would feel ever so much more comfortable were you to help me get out of these cumbersome rags," he said with a smile and a wink. With his wang to the wind, he took the ropes from the pile of clothes and looped them into slipknots.

"Hold out your lovely little feet, Dove," he coaxed. "Your ankles are asking to be captured."

"So they are," Ping agreed. "Won't you please accommodate them?"

Men attached the end of each rope to each of those delightful little ankles and the other ends to upright poles that supported the arbor. Ping's legs were thus spread wide apart and elevated. Her trimmed love-flower now adorned the center of the arbor for her swain's viewing delight.

Men knelt between the outspread legs and bowed his head reverently towards the single flowered bouquet. He spread the labial petals apart and lavishly kissed the moist fragrant offering. As he sucked and licked fervently, he extended his arms so his hands reached his nymph's rosy-tipped breasts.

The combination of Men's slurping at her crotch and his pinching and squeezing of her nipples caused a great welling up of passion throughout Ping's lovely body. The juices at her lower orifice began to gush, to the sensual delight of her sylvan lover. She squirmed as much as possible in her bonded condition.

She ran her fingers through Men's hair, digging into his scalp with loving massaging motions. Holding his head tenderly into her saddle, she bumped and ground, smearing her love-juice all over his welcoming face.

The increased flow of her female love-juice was a clear cry to his turgid member to plunge itself into the depths of her womb. He scrunched forward and upward until his lips met her mouth and his courser grazed her moist mound.

As his tongue shot into her waiting mouth, Men thrust his palpitating minaret into the gurgling canyon of desire, up to the very hilt. Ping's arms encircled his body and her nails ran up and down his spine as he increased the tempo of his thrusts to a frenzy. Her love channel became pneumatic, sucking his ram-rod even deeper into her feminine mysteries.

Just as his climax was about to culminate the ecstasy, Hsi Men caught sight of Pink Aster arriving with a second flagon of wine that had been sent out by the cook for the couple's additional drinking pleasure. The sight of the lovely maiden at that moment only enhanced his pleasure as Men shot his wad into his convulsing partner in rapture.

Pink Aster set the flagon on the ground, and – embarrassed – turned to leave.

"Stay right there!" the master ordered.

But the maid was frightened, and even though the master had ordered her to stay, she ran off to her mistress's pavilion.

And there, in the privacy of the pavilion, she went to the closet where she knew her mistress kept a set of varied-sized ivory dildos. She amused herself by applying her favorite one to her favorite spot.

In the meantime, Men released Ping from her bonds and the two, still naked, went to the pavilion.

They looked in the window and saw the maid wrapped up in her masturbatory games. They did not disturb her but remained watching as they masturbated each other standing outside, peering in the window.

THREE'S COMPANY

Hsi Men's newfound revels with Number Six Wife were very satisfying, of course. But not to the extent of taming his rampant promiscuity.

Before long, he was roaming the streets of the city every evening, searching for new adventures.

One evening, he paid a visit to Mother Wong's tearoom. And when the crone spied him, she had an interesting suggestion for his consideration. For a price, of course. Hsi Men was a canny businessman. He understood business.

He slipped her six pieces of silver.

"I presume you are looking for a new field to plow," the old woman suggested.

"I do not wish my plow to get rusty," Master Hsi answered.

"I have a lady in mind for you," Mother Wong said forthrightly. "No sense beating around the proverbial bush, is there?

"However, she is not a virgin. If you must have a virgin at this time, I'll have to return this silver to you."

"I am not in the virgin seduction vein," Master Hsi admitted.

"Keep the silver. And, if your counsel results in a successful adventure, I assure you more silver will follow."

"The lady I am thinking of for you is twenty-three years old and happily married. I am a fair judge of female pulchritude. She is a petite little thing. A true doll, in my estimation. She is not at all sophisticated. One would even say she has simple country ways about her. But, from all signs that I can see, she has an honest, passionate nature. All in all, I – myself – find her lovely."

"I have always trusted your taste, Mother Wong," Men replied. "Pray continue."

"As providence would have it," the crone said with a wry smile, "she is the wife of one of your employees, Han Ko."

"Most excellent," Men exclaimed. "Ko is at present on his way to the imperial capital, accompanying one of my negotiators on a bit of business for me. He will be absent for a while."

"All to the good," Mother Wong agreed.

"The young lady's name is Yatao. And, from what I have observed, I believe she is already lonely for her husband and would welcome generous male solace."

"As you say, Mother, all to the good."

"As you may or may not know," Mother Wong told him, "the Hans live in a simple bungalow just a few blocks from here on Oxhide Alley."

"Might you be paying her a visit, soon?" Men asked.

"It would be the neighborly thing to do," the crafty ancient answered.

"I must be on my way," Men told her. "But I plan to come back to the teahouse here for a mid-afternoon tea."

"I believe I may have news of a tasty dish for you, on your return, Master Hsi," the old woman winked.

"I will look forward to it," the gentleman said with a smile as he rose and left the premises.

Not too long after Master Hsi left the teahouse, Mother Wong paid a friendly visit to Mistress Yatao.

"You must be rather lonely, Dear, with your husband away now," she said solicitously to her neighbor.

"Yes, Mother," the young lady said. "He has to travel a good deal in the service of his employer. He's been gone for a couple of weeks already – and won't be back for at least another month."

"You need company, my dear," the crone sympathized. "It is not good for a young lady to grieve for her missing husband in solitude."

"It *does* get lonely here in my little bungalow," Yatao said, beginning to get a feel for where things might be drifting.

"I know a gentleman who is also lonely," Mother Wong told her. "I was talking with him in the tearoom recently. Poor fellow is desolately lonely. Perhaps you would like to meet him."

"Is the gentleman some ugly old tightwad?" Yatao asked, picking up the thread with interest.

"Oh, not at all," Mother Wong told her. "He is quite handsome and just a few years older than you. Oh, and by the way. He happens to be very rich and quite generous."

"What else can you tell me about him?" the young housewife asked.

"The other thing about him of interest," the old lady said with a cagy smile, "is that you know him." Yatao was taken by surprise.

"You must be mistaken, Mother Wong," she exclaimed. "I do not know any gentleman who fits that description."

"Oh, I don't mean you know him personally," Mother Wong corrected herself. "I doubt that you have ever met him personally. But you know very well who he is."

"Don't keep me in suspense," Yatao cried. "Tell me who this man is."

"Master Hsi Men," the old lady said, laughing.

Yatao laughed with her.

"My dear husband's employer?"

"The very same."

Yatao had seen Master Hsi from a distance, but their social positions were such that they had never actually met. She knew that Master Hsi was rich and handsome. And Mother Wong said he was generous.

The young beauty told her kind neighbor she would not be averse to meeting the lonely gentleman the following noon.

When Master Hsi returned to the teahouse mid-afternoon, the proprietress did, indeed, have a nice surprise to offer along with the oolong tea.

"A tasty dish awaits your pleasure at noon tomorrow on Oxhide Alley," she told him as she set a tea service before him on the table.

He paid for the tea and laid down six talents of silver as well.

"Speaking of dishes," he said. "It would be appreciated if a full basket of delicacies was awaiting my visit. Wine, fruit, meat, cakes and even – perhaps – a bottle of baijiu."

"All will be in readiness, I assure you," Mother Wong promised him, dropping the silver into her receptacle.

She told the rakehell exactly how to locate the bungalow on Oxhide Alley and told him Mistress Yatao would be awaiting his visit at noon the following day.

Master Hsi arrived at the modest house of his employee's wife precisely on time the next day.

When Mistress Yatao met him at the rear door, Master Hsi was absolutely delighted. The diminutive beauty was all that the old procuress had suggested. And more.

When he entered the modest house, he was happy to see that it was spotlessly clean. A table that served as a kind of buffet was laid out with an assortment of delicacies, a bottle of wine, and a bottle of baijiu.

There was, of course, no servant in the house. Servants did not exist in Oxhide Alley.

Yatao asked him if he would care for a cup of tea. Although Men would have liked to get right down to some heavier drinking, he followed protocol and accepted the invitation to join his hostess for tea. She had water already boiling and had the tea steeping in minutes as her guest made himself comfortable at the simple functional table.

After tea, traditional formalities and polite aimless conversation, Mistress Yatao brought wine goblets and tasty delicacies to the table. Master Hsi suggested they share just one goblet. Mistress Yatao acquiesced. And they drank their wine from the same side of the goblet.

Master Hsi rose from the table to get the bottle of baijiu from the buffet table. He brought it back to the dinner table and poured. When he sat down, his hostess moved her chair closer to his so they abutted.

Each took a sip of the fiery liquor he had poured. He placed a hand on her back and another behind her head and brought her lips to his. As soon as their lips met, she inserted her tongue into his mouth. He sucked her tongue with passionate expertise. As he continued sucking, her hand fell onto his thigh. As it crept up into his lap, it met an erect pole.

Men did not let up on his attention to her tongue as his right hand found purchase on her breast. In accordance with her diminutive size, it was a small, delicate and perfect globe.

By mutual unspoken agreement, they both doffed their clothing.

Men lifted her light, smooth-skinned body in his bare muscular arms and bore her to the adjacent bedroom. He laid her down atop the rough sheets and gazed down on her. He was stunned by the perfection of her thin, lithe body. He felt that he had never before beheld such loveliness. Yatao's face was a picture of classic Chinese exquisiteness. Her perky breasts were in perfect proportion to her miniature body. On her pubes lay a black-blue, silky, perfect triangle that pointed to a raised mound of loveliness. And her feet, though unbound, were tiny and perfect.

And the fragrance from her armpits and moist outspread thighs, unenhanced by perfumes or oils, had a natural headiness that inflamed his passion.

The figure spread out before him was the essential female, the natural unsophisticated form created without adornment to seduce a male's very soul.

Master Hsi reflected briefly on the seductive charms of his wives. And he saw them as creatures artificially employing female wiles to pleasure their mate. The pure woman before him was there to satisfy her own primal urges. And by yielding to those urges, she would give him a satisfaction undimmed by urbanity.

As he settled onto the bed beside her, there was a frantic urgency to her response. The light finger strokes he ran up and down her body elicited shivers and convulsions in her responsive body.

Kissing her small cherry lips caused her lungs to inspire deeply, sweeping his own tongue into her anticipating mouth. And with that sweep, there was the promise of a later similar sweep of his virile member into that tight little oral cavity.

With her delicate hands, Yatao guided his hips up and over her own so that his courser would inevitably descend into her moist waiting love-saddle.

Her cries and screams of joy filled Men's ears with tremendous satisfaction. She was sensitive to his least thrust, whether he was slithering his poker around inside her or threatening to extract it and then slyly re-lunging. He thrilled to the way her antic hands and fingernails frantically clawed and scratched his back. When he slid a finger around her body and into her bung, she squeezed her labia down to the very base of his pole.

As he felt himself nearing his climax, she withdrew her treasure box from his red-hot pole and – leaving a trail of her feminine moisture down his thighs and legs – she slid down to suck the spongy head of his organ, drawing the cream from his scrotum up into the cavern behind her tiny mouth. When he collapsed onto the sheets beside her, she reached out to cradle his testicles in her hand. He reciprocated by kneading and twisting her nipples until they were strained out in two lovely pink towers.

It was not long before his phoenix had risen again. When it was turgid, he slipped down the bed to where he faced directly into her love-box. She grabbed his hair and guided his face over her thighs to where his lips and tongue could make purchase on her tight little garden gate.

Men parted the outer lips of her nether mouth and inserted his tongue into the sea-scented paradise at his disposal. With sucking and licking around her clitoris and around the rim of the entrance, and by persistent probing with his flickering tongue, he brought her just short of a moaning climax.

Yatao pulled her lover up onto her body by the hair and guided his pulsating member into the tiny hole that clenched itself tightly around his staff.

When they came, neither could mute the cries that arose spontaneously from their throats. Their utterances were far more animal than human.

For the entire afternoon and into the evening, the courser roared back into motion. During the necessary recesses they took, they finished off the wine, liquor and foodstuffs from the improvised buffet table.

Hsi Men left an abundance of silver behind when he departed the next morning. It was understood that Yatao was to suffer no want of any kind while the master kept her company during the time her husband was away.

Master Hsi was no stranger from then on at the bungalow on Oxhide Alley. Men promised to send a maid to the bungalow to assist his new love in any way she might choose. A true novelty for the neighborhood.

Twinkling Star moved in with Yatao before noon the next day.

In due time, Han Ko returned to his wife and home from his lengthy journey. Yatao was delighted to see him again and demonstrated her pleasure very much to her husband's satisfaction.

Ko told her in detail about his adventures along the road to the imperial capital. And about the wonders of the great bustling city. She ate up every word.

As Ko finished the tale of his wondrous voyage, he told her about a delightful thing that happened when he got back to the province.

"When Master Hsi's negotiator and I returned here, we – of course – went directly to see the master at his shop to give our reports.

"At the conclusion of the transaction, he unexpectedly gave me fifty talents of silver beyond my due. I, of course, protested three times, but he absolutely insisted. What a wonderful man he is to work for."

He turned the money over to Yatao to take care of. She was the one who had abilities in such household matters. Then Yatao told Ko one of the things she thought they should do with a portion of the windfall:

"We should give Mother Wong a talent of the silver," she said.

"The old lady was very kind to me and watched over my welfare while you were away. She consoled me in my loneliness."

Just then, Twinkling Star entered the room carrying a tray of tea and cakes. She set the tray on the table and kowtowed her new master.

"Who in the world is this?" Ko asked. Twinkling Star rose and returned to the kitchen.

It was Yatao's turn to explain to her husband how she – in that humble bungalow – could possibly now have a servant.

She knew her husband was a freethinker and was not a prude in any way. So she told him about how Mother Wong had introduced her to Master Hsi and how very profitable her relationship with the master had been.

"So now we not only have a servant," she informed him, "but Master Hsi also promised us a very nice house on Dragon Street. That is what the fifty talents were for. What do you think of that?"

Han Ko thought it was just wonderful.

"The silver will not stop there," she promised. "After we buy the house, more silver will come tumbling into our coffers. I won't mind him taking his pleasure with my body. It is quite

rewarding for us. And, besides, he is a very accomplished lover."
Ko smiled.

"If the master should drop by here tomorrow while I'm
off at work, do be a very gracious hostess," he advised his wife.
"Pretend that I don't know what's going on. And let the silver keep
flowing in."

The couple purchased a nice six-room home on Dragon
Street the following day.

And Hsi Men became a very welcome visitor to their new
abode.

Before long, Yatao let her lover know that her husband was
aware of their relationship. And that he was quite open-minded
about the whole matter. So Men no longer felt constrained to visit
Yatao only when her husband was absent.

Hsi Men was, of course, also open-minded. And he did not
object to Han Ko's presence in the house or in the bedroom, while
he and Yatao engaged in their bacchanals.

As a matter of fact, Men purchased a very comfortable couch
and had it placed against a wall of the room. Han Ko and Twinkling
Star occupied the couch on occasion to disport themselves while
the two lovers had their festive romps. The situation somehow
added spice to Men's frolics. And her husband's presence with the
maid did not seem to inhibit Yatao one bit. Occasionally, when
Twinkling Star was otherwise occupied, Ko entertained himself by
playing with his own lively toy as he watched his wife and his
employer engage in every position in the Jade Canon.

And the silver that kept pouring in was shrewdly invested
by Yatao where it was both safe and earning interest for her and her
husband.

NO ARMOR AGAINST KARMA

Then, one day, the idyllic relationship Hsi had with his mistress hit a snag. Men arrived at the house on Dragon Street during daylight hours while Ko was working at the shop.

Yatao met him as always, radiating smiles and exuding the lusty scent that emanated from her entire body. Men was especially stimulated by the natural female odor. And Yatao's fragrance was more enchanting to him than that of any woman he had ever known. Including Plum Blossom.

The master carried his dove into the bedroom and set her dainty feet down onto the floor. She stood before him and disrobed in her own provocative fashion. He was, as always, entranced.

Nude and resplendent, she dropped to her knees and pulled his trousers down. He stepped out of them.

Yatao then pulled down his small clothes, leaving his groin bare.

Bare. But, alas, unaroused.

The master's once proud dragon hung pitifully from his groin like a defunct rat. Tatao lifted the drooping creature and attempted to resuscitate it by abundant applications of saliva and deep engulfment of both the soft head and the flaccid staff. All to no avail. The miserable beast remained limp and totally unresponsive.

Hsi Men's alarm was intense. Whether Yatao dealt with the inert drooping staff or the sack of love-marbles descending from it – hands, fingers, lips, tongue and mouth availed it naught. He felt the accustomed tingles of desire. But they did not elevate the means of satisfying it. The member was tragically dead.

Yatao lay down on the bed and her erstwhile lover hovered above her outspread thighs, attempting to cram the recalcitrant staff into the quivering hole that anxiously awaited it. But the erstwhile monster refused to be forced into the cavern.

Men called out to Twinkling Star, ordering her into the bedroom. When she arrived, her mistress bade her disrobe. The maid complied willingly enough. Although she had been often bedded by her mistress's husband, she had thus far been denied the ministration of Master Hsi's erotic attention.

While the maid worked the master's groin with finger, hands and lips, her mistress lowered her nether parts down onto his face. Master Hsi avidly smacked at, kissed and tongued both the tasty orifices presented to his mouth. And he was acutely aware of what the lovely maid was about at his crotch. Yet, the total exercise was a humiliating disaster.

It was the most dreadful thing that the libertine had ever experienced in his entire life.

Impotent! Oh, the pain! The shame! The loss of the only thing in the world that makes life worth living!

In desperation, Men applied the technique he had so loved in his adolescence. But he found that masturbation was as useless a remedy to his dysfunction as the ministrations of his lover and the maid.

Hsi Men did not go home that night. He remained at the house on Dragon Street and drank himself into a case of extreme inebriation on baijiu. He passed out naked on the bed. Yatao slept next to him and Ko passed the night on the couch.

Men did not awaken the next morning until after Ko had left for work.

When he *did* awake, his headache was intense, his stomach was queasy and his balance was off. Yatao and Twinkling Star helped him bathe and get into his clothing. With difficulty, the master got some tea and rice cakes and headed for the Dao-xuan Buddhist monastery situated in the countryside not far outside the city wall.

When he entered the monastery, Men found an elderly, lean, emaciated monk sitting in solitary meditation before a statue of the Buddha. Hsi knew better than to disturb the holy man immersed in his morning practice. Men sat down next to the monk in the lotus position and waited for him to come out of his trance.

Master Hsi sat there for two hours before he heard the old man recite a sutra and arise.

The monk observed his companion with clear compassion.

"What brings the noble gentleman to the house of tranquility?" the old man asked.

"I have been told that your order has an understanding of medicine that goes beyond the everyday," Men told him. "I myself am a dispenser of herbs and pills. I am well aware of the limits of the products I dispense. And I know that an affliction that I am suffering from is not going to respond to the simple aphrodisiacs available to modern medical practice."

Master Cheng, for such was the holy man's name, understood immediately that this suppliant was suffering from impotence. And his natural compassion was further aroused.

"You are fortunate to know that the aphrodisiacs available in your lay world will not affect the condition which karma has settled on you," he told the herbalist. "And, in the course of your education, I imagine that you were informed that the Bodhisattva brought secret, ancient healing recipes to his followers."

Of course, Hsi Men had heard of such things. In desperation. That was why he had come to the monastery to seek a cure from his curse.

"I can offer you a cure for your lamentable situation," the monk said with a smile. "But, of course, there is a condition attached to my offer."

"I am a very rich man," Men informed Master Cheng. "Whatever price you ask, I can pay."

The Buddhist master's smile grew wider.

"Your riches will avail you nothing," he told him. "Only by taking a holy vow can you be led to the Cell of the Bo Tree Fruit."

A vow? Well, I can promise anything. And, if the medicine doesn't work, I can legally recant the vow. And if the medicine relieves me of my impotence, nearly anything will be worth it... Depending on the vow, of course.

"What, Master, would I have to promise?" Master Hsi asked.

"Once you are freed of the impotence you suffer, you will be free to live however you please. But, after a year, you must return here and live a life of poverty, abstinence and meditation for a full year. Else you will suffer worse than impotence for the rest of this life and the next one."

*Not a bad deal. I get back my erections and can live as
dissolute a life as I wish for a year. Then a year living as a Buddhist
monk will be worth it. After that, I get my life back. Deal!*

"I will accept your condition," he told Master Cheng.

So, bowing before the stature of the Buddha, Master Hsi
Men repeated the vow in the words that the ancient monk provided
for him. He repeated the five holy sutras of devotion to the Buddha.
Then he followed the monk to the Bo Tree Cell.

The cell was stocked with an unbelievable abundance of
herbs and other medications. None of them was recognizable to
the professional herbalist.

So *this* was the magical stash of the disciples of Bodhisattva.

The monk handed the suppliant an earthenware plate. Men
received it with his arms outstretched, kneeling before Master
Cheng on both knees. Master Cheng measured out three-hundred-
sixty-five green pills, one at a time.

"You will take one pill each day. Never more than one, mind
you. And you must wash the pill down with pure spring water."

Men emptied the contents of the tray into his purse. Master
Cheng then brought forth a jar of red salve.

"You must sanctify your torpid member with this salve
carefully before any kind of carnal experience," he advised. "Apply
it very sparingly, never more than the amount you can smear lightly
on the nail of your little finger. But be warned, my son. Do not
exceed taking but one pill a day. And you must never apply more
than a very minute amount of the salve to your member."

"What effect will the pill and the salve have on me?" Men
asked.

"Your potency will exceed anything you have known
before," he was told. "No woman, not even a bevy of women, can
outlast your potency. However, if you feel a depletion of energy

during an encounter, a drink of spring water will revive you. Always have a container with you."

Men kowtowed before the monk, added the container of salve to his pouch, promised to return in a year to fulfill his vow, and left the monastery a very happy man indeed.

He proceeded to his shop, because among the items he dispensed from, there were very fine containers of water secured from the best springs in the empire. He picked up a large container and, with the items he had brought with him from the monastery, he proceeded directly to Dragon Street to enjoy the benefits to be derived from the Bo Tree Cell.

From the expression on her lover's face when he arrived at the door, Yatao divined that he had discovered a remedy for his dysfunction. She led him into the bedroom where they both hastily disrobed. He popped a green pill, swigged a mouthful of water and applied a minute quantity of a red colored salve to his slack member.

The flagpole sprang up with such a bound that both Men and Yatao jumped up in amazement. It pulsed with wild anticipation of good times ahead. Men wrapped his arms around his lover's back and yanked her forward so her cherry lips were pressed tightly against his muscled chest. She felt his throbbing dragon beat a tattoo against her midriff that kept time to his pounding heartbeat. She responded instantly to his fervor. His fingers launched into the wetness between her thighs and she shuddered with passion.

His hands scooted around to her buttocks, lifted her off the ground and positioned her receptive vulva to his wild stallion.

As he lowered her down – skewering her front entrance – the tiny hole that crowned the head of his rod spewed a discharge into the channel it was entering. Yatao was so stimulated that she responded with an orgasm of her own.

Men lifted her in his arms and carried her to the bed. As he laid her down, both he and she were delighted to discover that his erection had not subsided.

He re-entered the garden of delights and thrusted and pounded the receiving saddle to the delight of both of them.

And, once again, the action milked the contents of his scrotum.

Following every discharge of semen, his scrotum immediately was replenished with a new supply. And his libido was recharged.

Yatao's lips sought the satisfaction of sucking at Men's unquenchable fountainhead. She thirstily approached the curiously recharged source and swallowed the cream past her tiny rosebud of a mouth and slipped the shaft as far as it would reach into her throat.

The rock-hard pillar spurted jet after jet into her swanlike throat. She swallowed the love-juice with delight.

When Men withdrew from her oral cavity, they both realized that Yatao still had an unfulfilled orifice. But, alas, Men's robust organ began to lose some of its uprightness.

In a state not unlike intoxication, Men threw caution to the winds. He grabbed a couple of the miracle pills, washed them down with spring water and applied a bit more salve to the wilting stallion. The result was immediate. The monster rose to a new life and within seconds had found Yatao's anus. Both of the participants howled with delight as the brave new warrior launched into the breach.

That final assault turned out to be too much for Yatao. She collapsed in bliss and exhaustion onto the drenched sheets.

Men was now insatiable in appetite and mad with lust. He had to find release for the intensity of his libido. He hastily got into his clothes, and – forsaking his burned-out paramour – headed directly to the Flower Garden District to find Cinnamon Petal.

He burst into her house only to find her engaged with a customer. In a fury, he lifted the nude man out of the bed and tossed him out the window. Then, downing a pill and taking a swig of his water and anointing his rod with a generous application of salve, he assaulted Cinnamon Bud's already moistened fissure.

Even though she was an experienced tow girl, his intensity overcame her and she collapsed from the encounter.

Now in the District, Hsi Men rushed from one to another of the establishments he had previously frequented. In his sex-crazed madness, he fed his quest with pill after pill and slathered his pole with the energizing salve. Panic seized the District. Screaming women fled through the streets and alleys of the neighborhood in horror.

He then headed for home. When he arrived, he proceeded desperately to Plum Blossom's pavilion.

She was delighted to see him, for she had been craving a little action. She helped him out of his clothes, since he appeared to have lost the coordination to do the job himself.

She undressed and put him onto the bed.

She grew furious when he fell asleep on her.

She shook him awake.

Rubbing her nether lips with a moist finger, she shouted in his ear, "Wake up, you fool. Don't you dare go back to sleep on me. I need some action."

"I'm so tired," he mumbled. "I'm afraid I can't service you unless you can get some of those little green pills from my satchel. And some of the water in the container. And the red salve for my…"

Plum Blossom hurried to get into her husband's satchel. And there she found pills, water and salve.

She wanted action and was happy to give Men whatever it took to get him frisky again. So she gave him a handful of pills to swallow. He dutifully got them down. She slathered her hands with the salve and liberally coated his manhood and scrotum with it.

Alas! The treatment did not restore Master Hsi. He fainted dead away, and there was no reviving him.

The next morning, Plum Blossom still could not wake him. She called for Dr. Lau to come.

When Dr. Lau examined Master Hsi, his penis had shriveled, his testicles had swollen and his scrotum was inflamed. The doctor knew of no medicine to provide for the lamentable condition of the hollow-cheeked, near-corpse on the bed.

And on the third month of his forty-third year, Master Hsi Men's soul departed his body.

AFTERWORD

When a year had passed, Master Cheng waited for Hsi Men's return to the monastery to fulfill his vow. When the suppliant failed to appear, the old monk sighed in compassion.

He stepped outside the monastery's portals and read again the writing engraved above the entry.

Bodhisattva's famous maxim was engraved there for all to read…:

There is no armor against karma

LAST WORDS

Western readers tend to be dissatisfied with the ending Lanling Xianxiao Shen gave to his masterpiece. We tend to want to know what fate awaited Plum Blossom. Buddhist and Hindu readers seem not to be perplexed at all.

To them, the book is a moralistic novel. And the final words, which are Bodhisattva's maxim, are sufficient to presage what happened to Hsi Men's Number Six Wife.

ABOUT THE AUTHOR

Tim Desmondes

Tim Desmondes and his wife reside in Southern California. Tim is the author of twelve books other than the present volume published by The Nazca Plains Corporation.

- *Sex and Loathing in Hollywood* (March, '08)
- *Sexual Diversity and Perversity in California* (March, '08)
- *Dracula Sucks Hollywood Dudes* (April, '08)
- *Venus Does Adonis While Apollo Shags a Tree* (May, '08)
- *Arthur Does Camelot* (September, '08)
- *Whores, Love and Pistols in the Wild West* (September, '08)
- *Robin's Too Tight Tights* (November, '08)
- *Sex and Love in Paris and Frisco* (January, '09)
- *Beowulf, Wulfgar and Their Friggin Horny Gods* (May, '09)

- *Colleen O'Merry – Dominatrix to the Starts* (September, '10)
- *Wanda the Whip Lady* (October, '10)
- *Agnes Sorel* (August, '11)

If *Plum Blossom's Fragrant Loins* tickled your fancy, you will probably enjoy some of his other ribald stories.

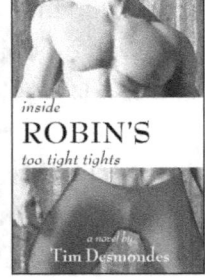

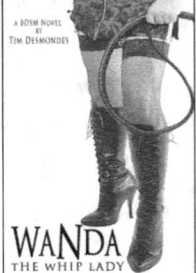